BENNY AND PENNY

IN

LOST and
FOUND!

GEOFFREY HAYES

BENNY AND PENNY
IN
LOST AND FOUND!

PENNY!

A TOON BOOK BY

GEOFFREY HAYES

TOON BOOKS IS AN IMPRINT OF CANDLEWICK PRESS

A JUNIOR LIBRARY GUILD SELECTION
KIRKUS BEST CONTINUING SERIES

Make sure to find all the Benny and Penny books:

Benny and Penny in Just Pretend

Benny and Penny in The Toy Breaker

Benny and Penny in Lights Out!

Benny and Penny in The Big No-No!, A GEISEL AWARD WINNER!

Editorial Director: FRANÇOISE MOULY

Book Design: FRANÇOISE MOULY & JONATHAN BENNETT

GEOFFREY HAYES' artwork was done in colored pencil.

A TOON Book™ © 2014 Geoffrey Hayes & RAW Junior, LLC, 27 Greene Street, New York, NY 10013. TOON Books is an imprint of Candlewick Press, 99 Dover Street, Somerville, MA 02144. No part of this book may be used or reproduced in any manner whatsoever without written permission except in the case of brief quotations embodied in critical articles and reviews. TOON Books®, LITTLE LIT®, and TOON Into Reading™ are trademarks of RAW Junior, LLC. All rights reserved.

Printed in China by C&C Offset Printing Co., Ltd.

Library of Congress Cataloging-in-Publication Data:

Hayes, Geoffrey.

Benny and Penny in Lost and found : a TOON book / by Geoffrey Hayes.   pages cm.   —(Easy-to-read comics. Level 2)

SUMMARY: Penny the mouse tries to help her brother Benny find his favorite hat, but Benny warns her that he is in a bad mood.

ISBN 978-1-935179-64-1(hardcover)

1. Graphic novels. [1. Graphic novels. 2. Lost and found possessions–Fiction. 3. Mood (Psychology)–Fiction. 4. Brothers and sisters–Fiction. 5. Mice–Fiction.] I. Title. II. Title: Lost and found.   PZ7.7.H39Bd 2014   741.5'973–dc23   2014000649

14 15 16 17 18 19 C&C 10 9 8 7 6 5 4 3 2 1

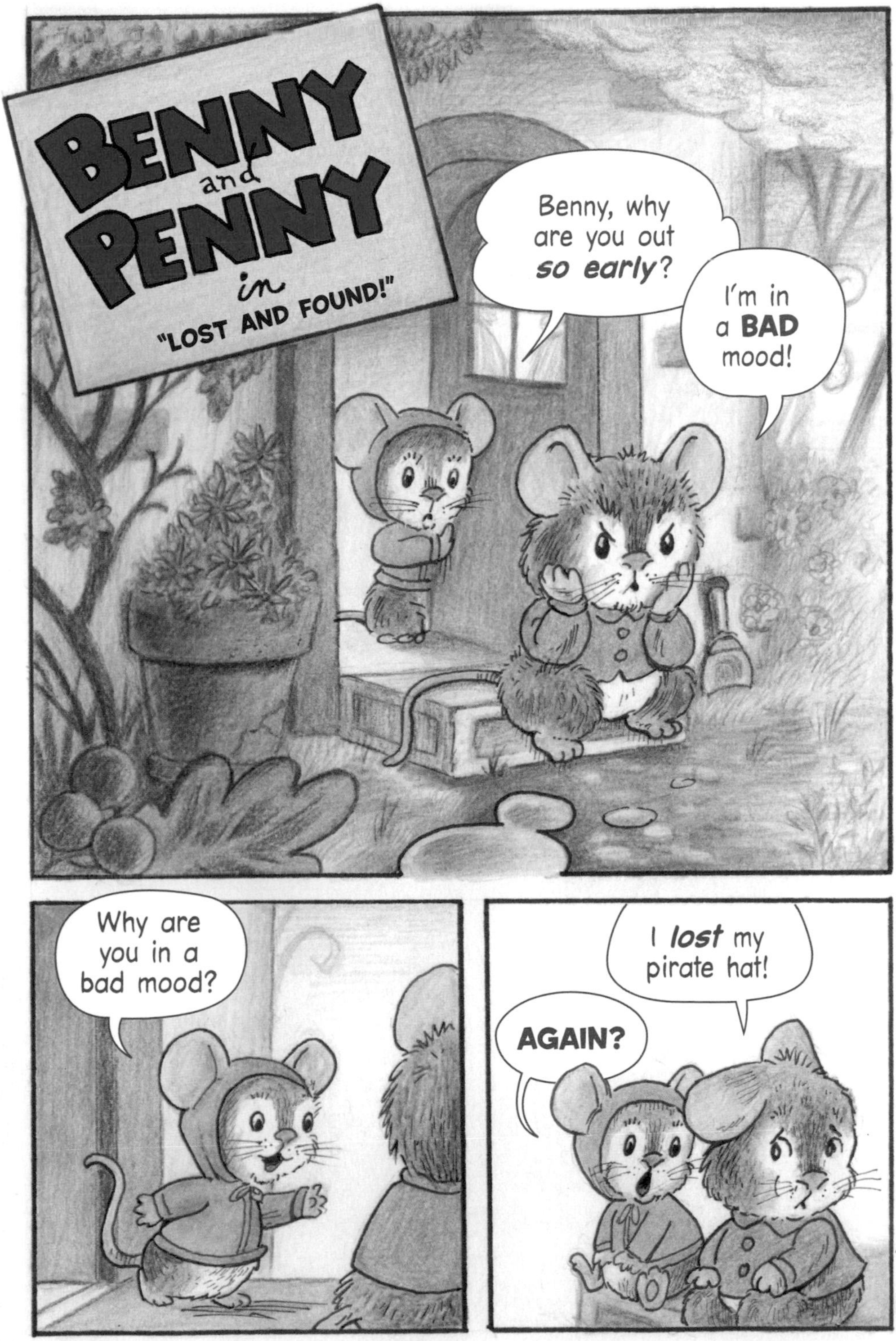
BENNY and PENNY in
"LOST AND FOUND!"
Benny, why are you out *so early*?
I'm in a **BAD** mood!
Why are you in a bad mood?
I *lost* my pirate hat!
AGAIN?

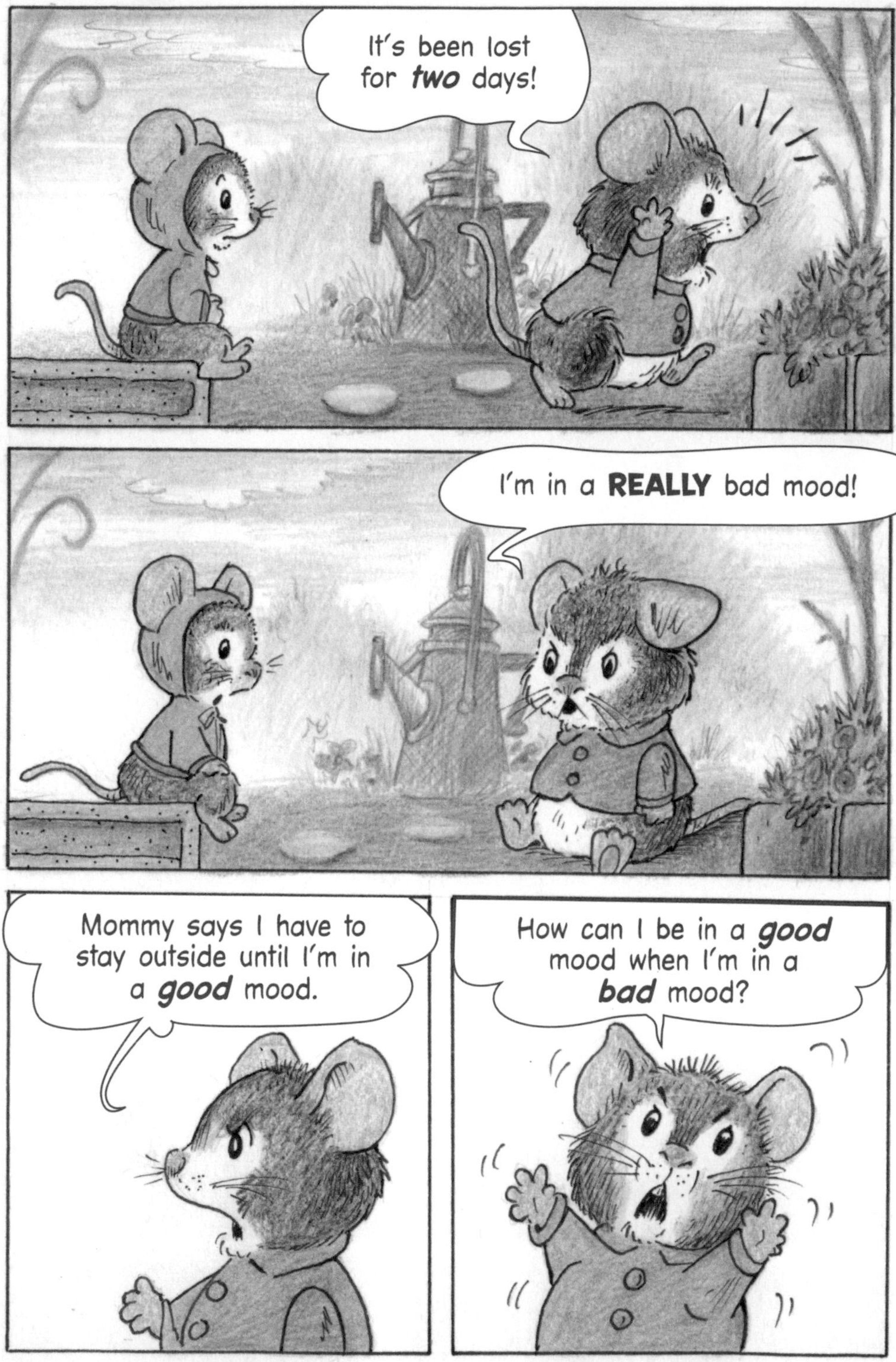
It's been lost for *two* days!
I'm in a **REALLY** bad mood!
Mommy says I have to stay outside until I'm in a *good* mood.
How can I be in a *good* mood when I'm in a *bad* mood?

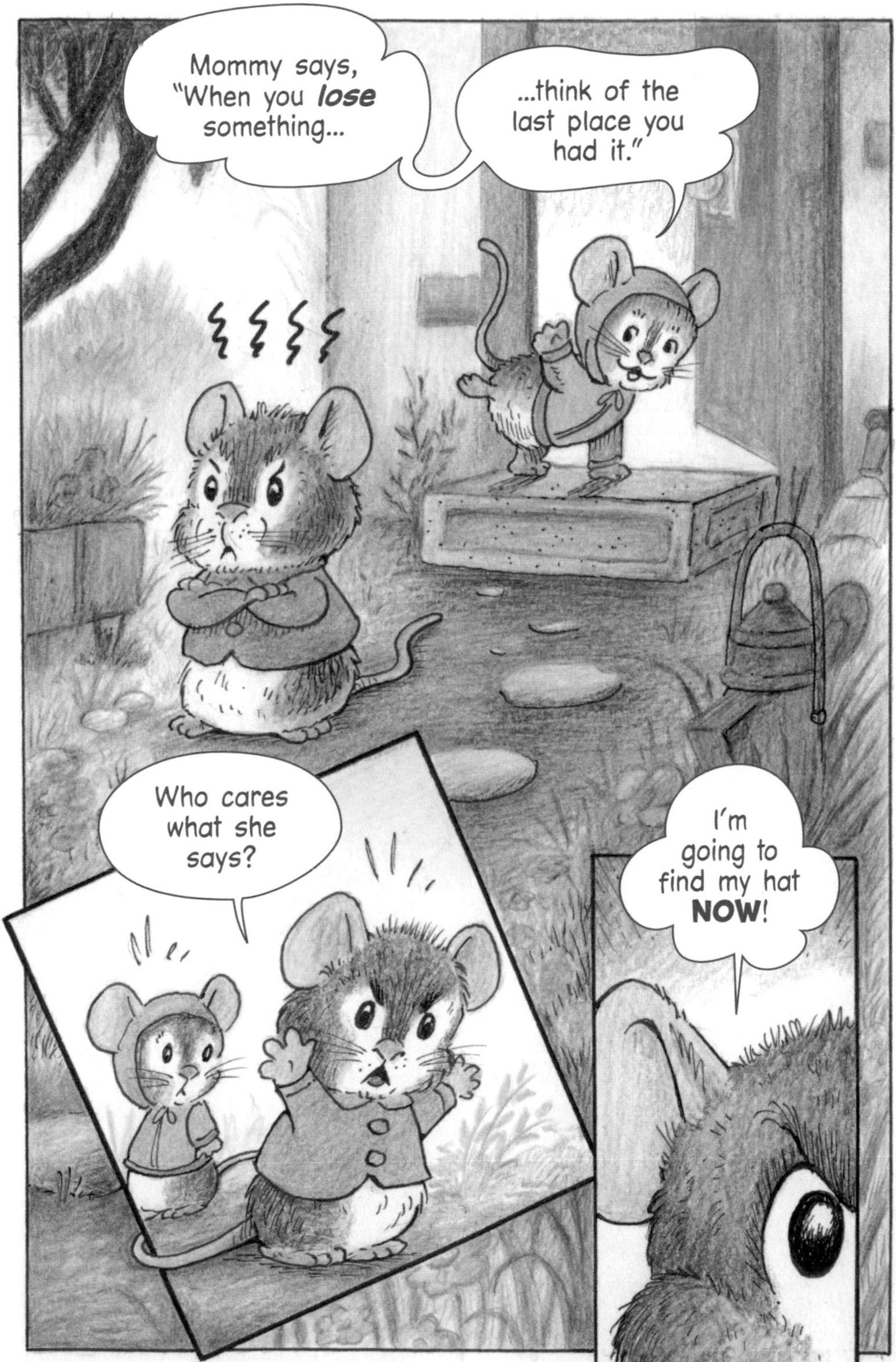
Mommy says, "When you ***lose*** something...
...think of the last place you had it."
Who cares what she says?
I'm going to find my hat **NOW**!

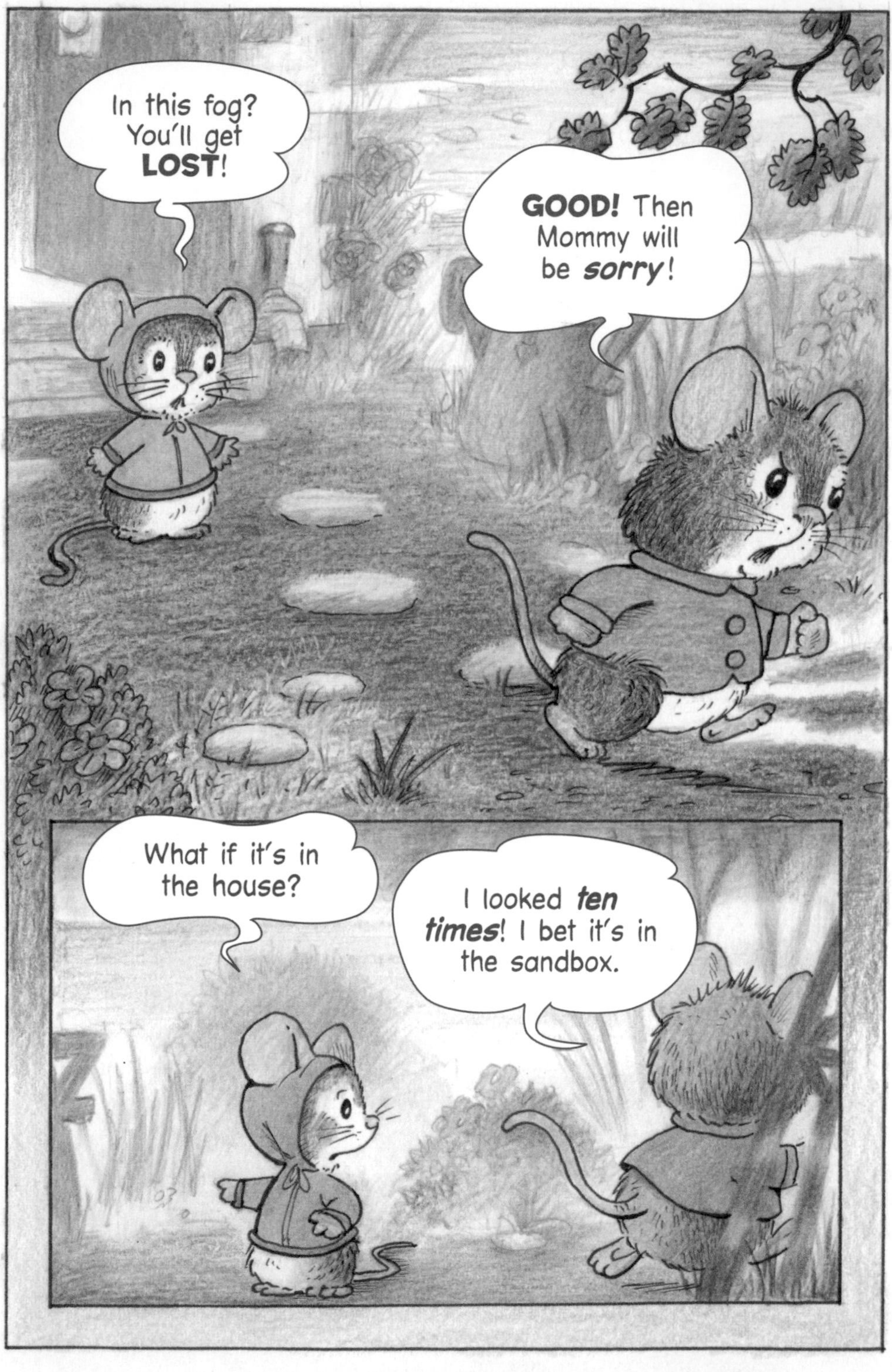
In this fog? You'll get **LOST**!
GOOD! Then Mommy will be ***sorry***!
What if it's in the house?
I looked ***ten times***! I bet it's in the sandbox.

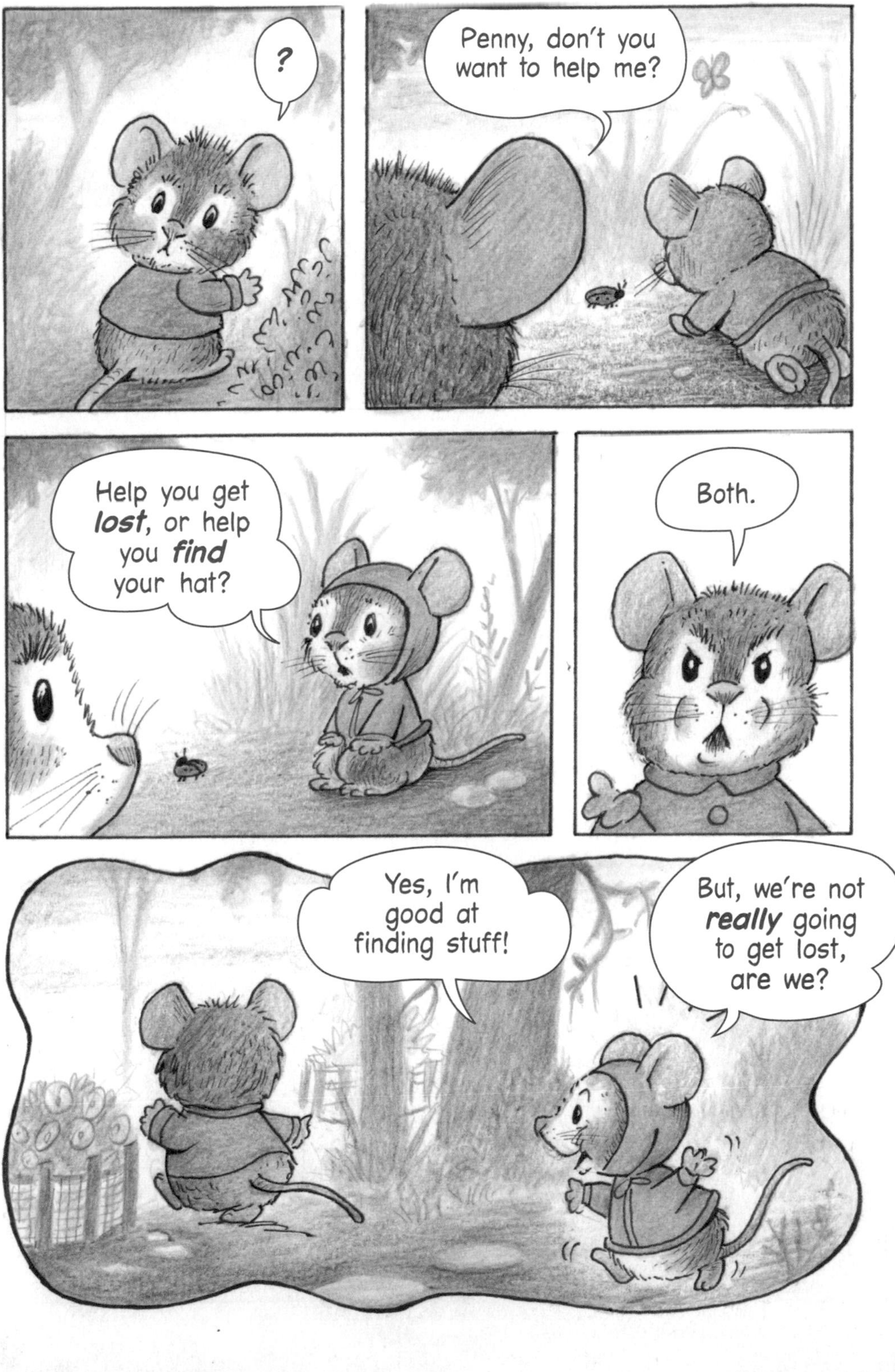
?
Penny, don't you want to help me?
Help you get *lost*, or help you *find* your hat?
Both.
Yes, I'm good at finding stuff!
But, we're not *really* going to get lost, are we?

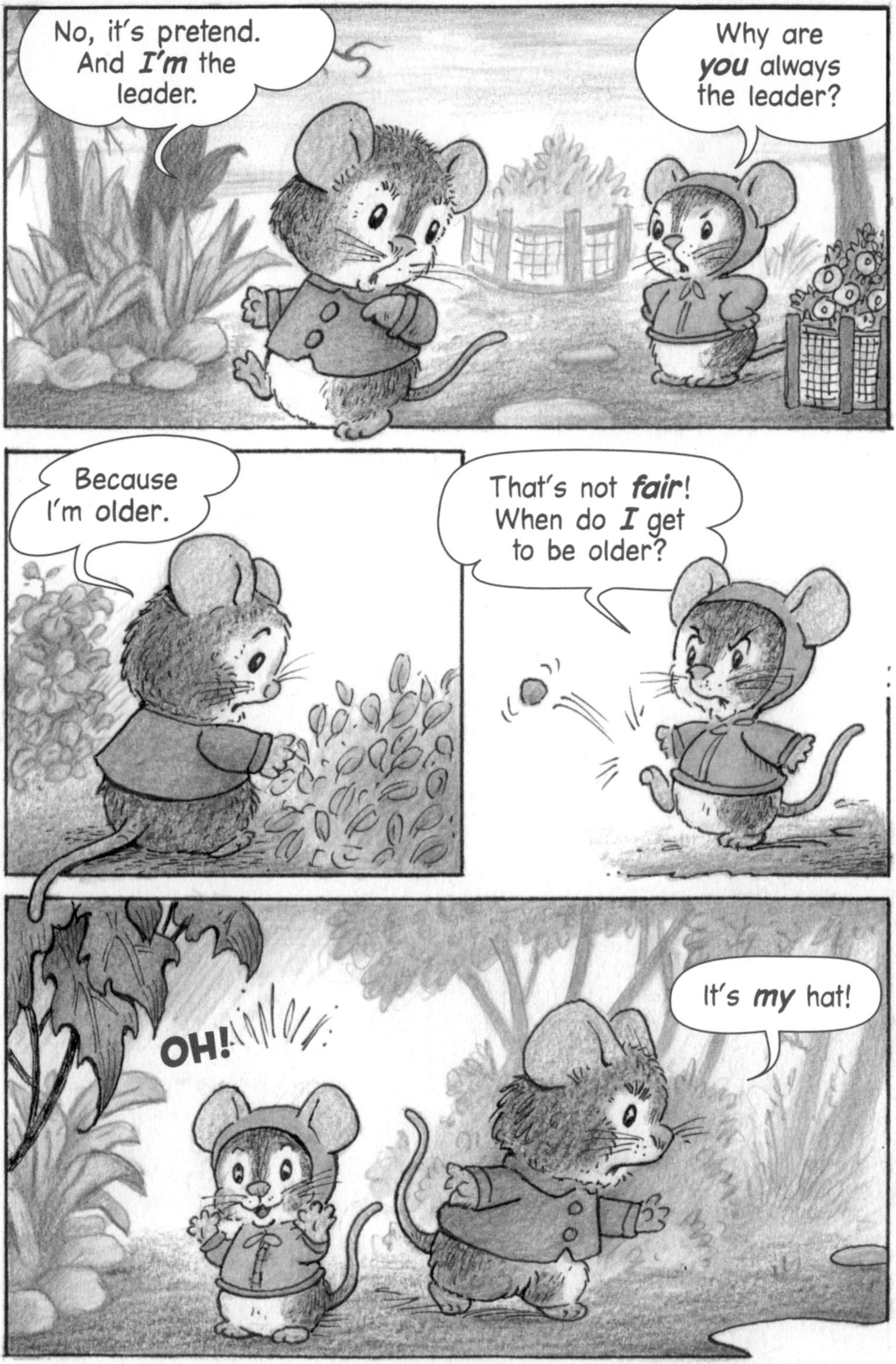
No, it's pretend. And *I'm* the leader.
Why are *you* always the leader?
Because I'm older.
That's not *fair*! When do *I* get to be older?
OH!
It's *my* hat!

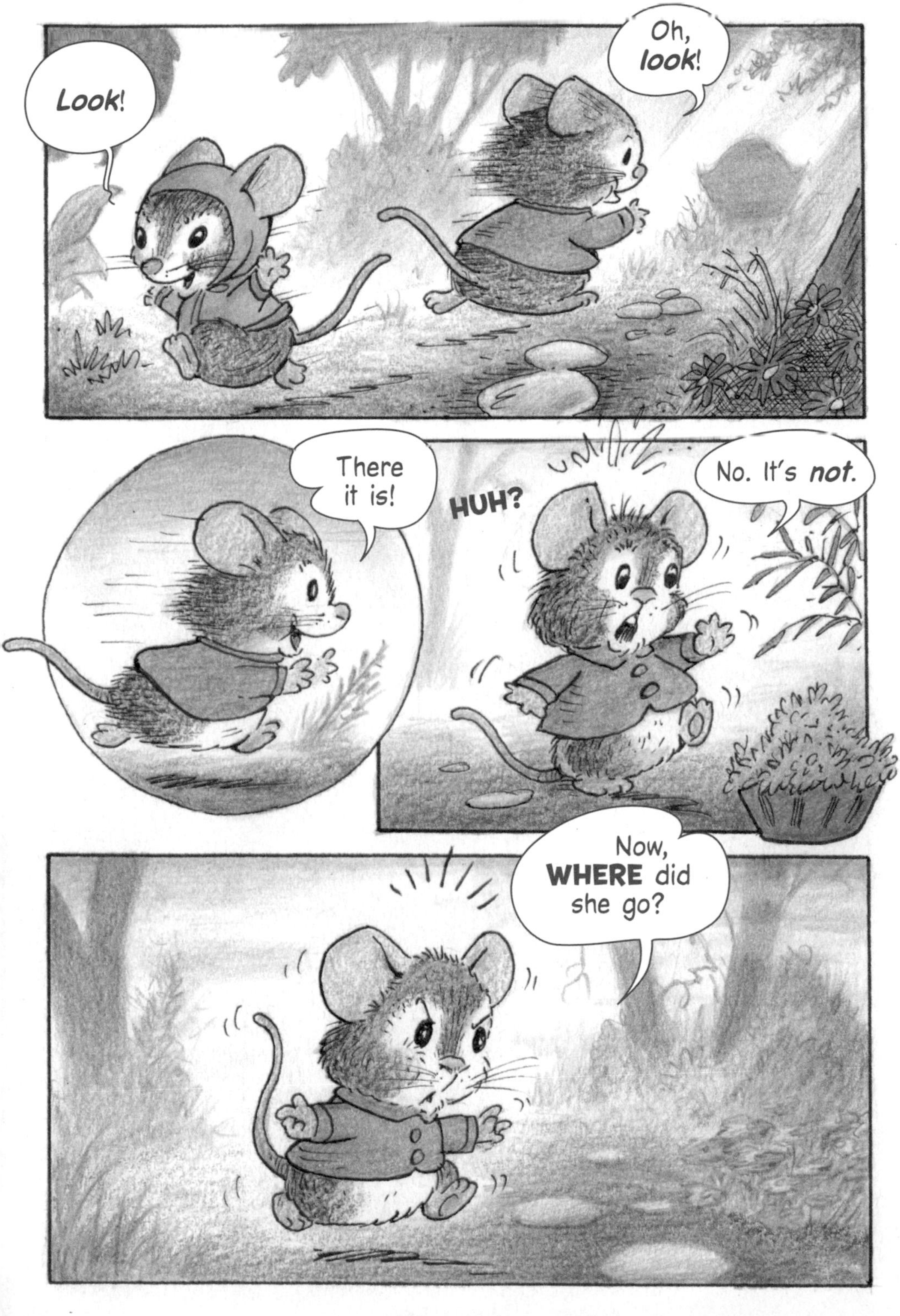
Look!
Oh, look!
There it is!
HUH?
No. It's not.
Now, WHERE did she go?

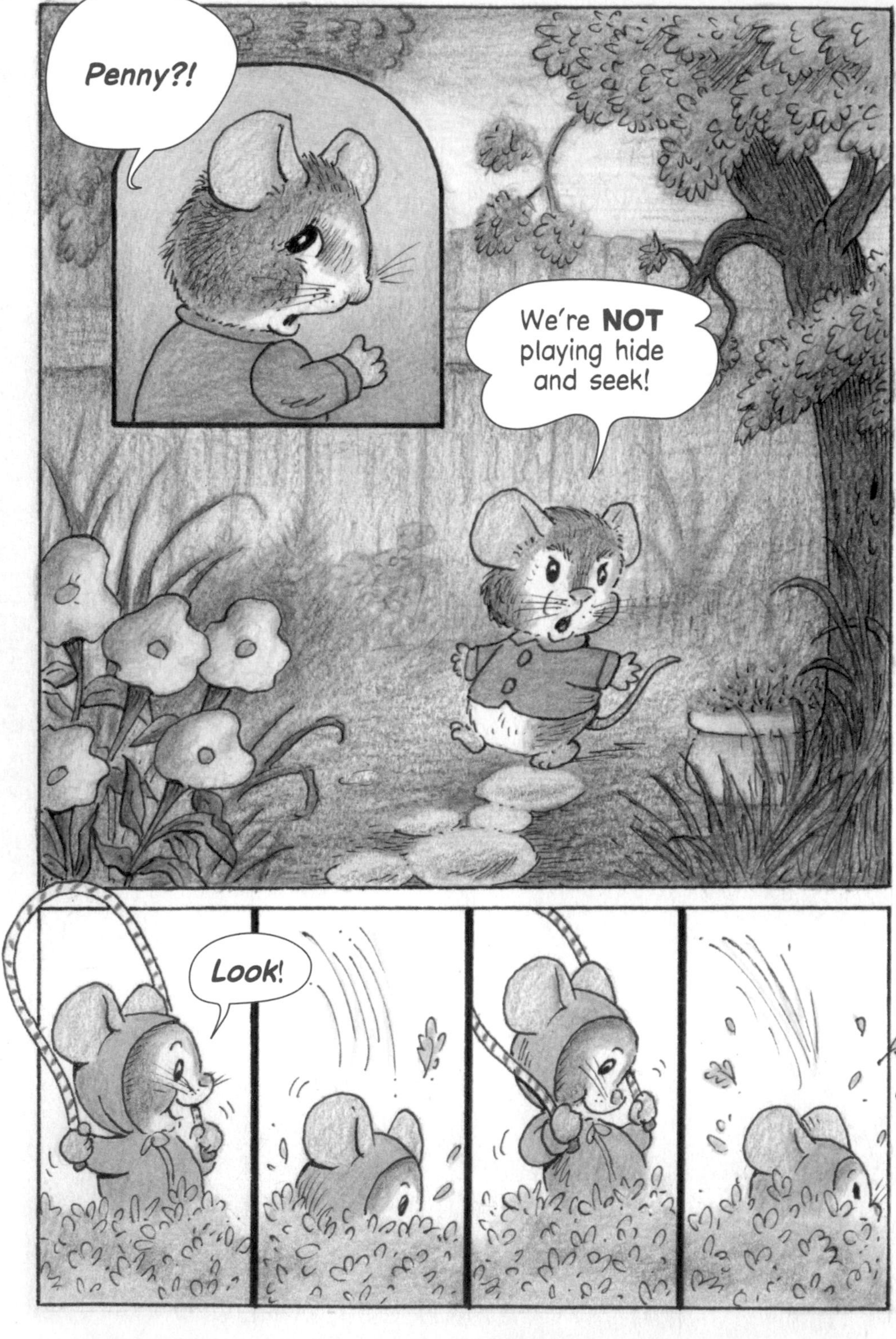
Penny?!
We're **NOT** playing hide and seek!
Look!

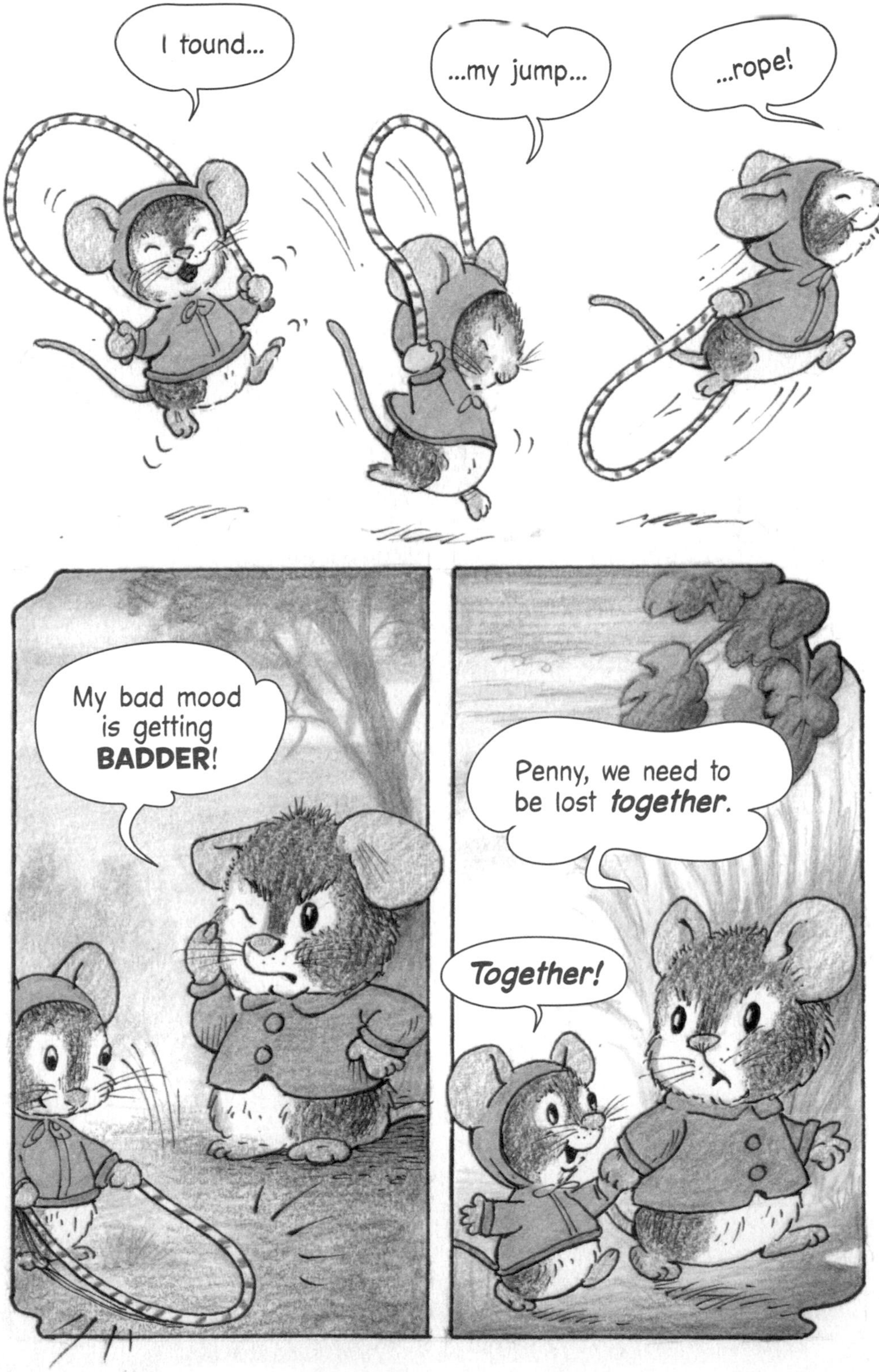
I found...
...my jump...
...rope!
My bad mood is getting **BADDER**!
Penny, we need to be lost *together*.
Together!

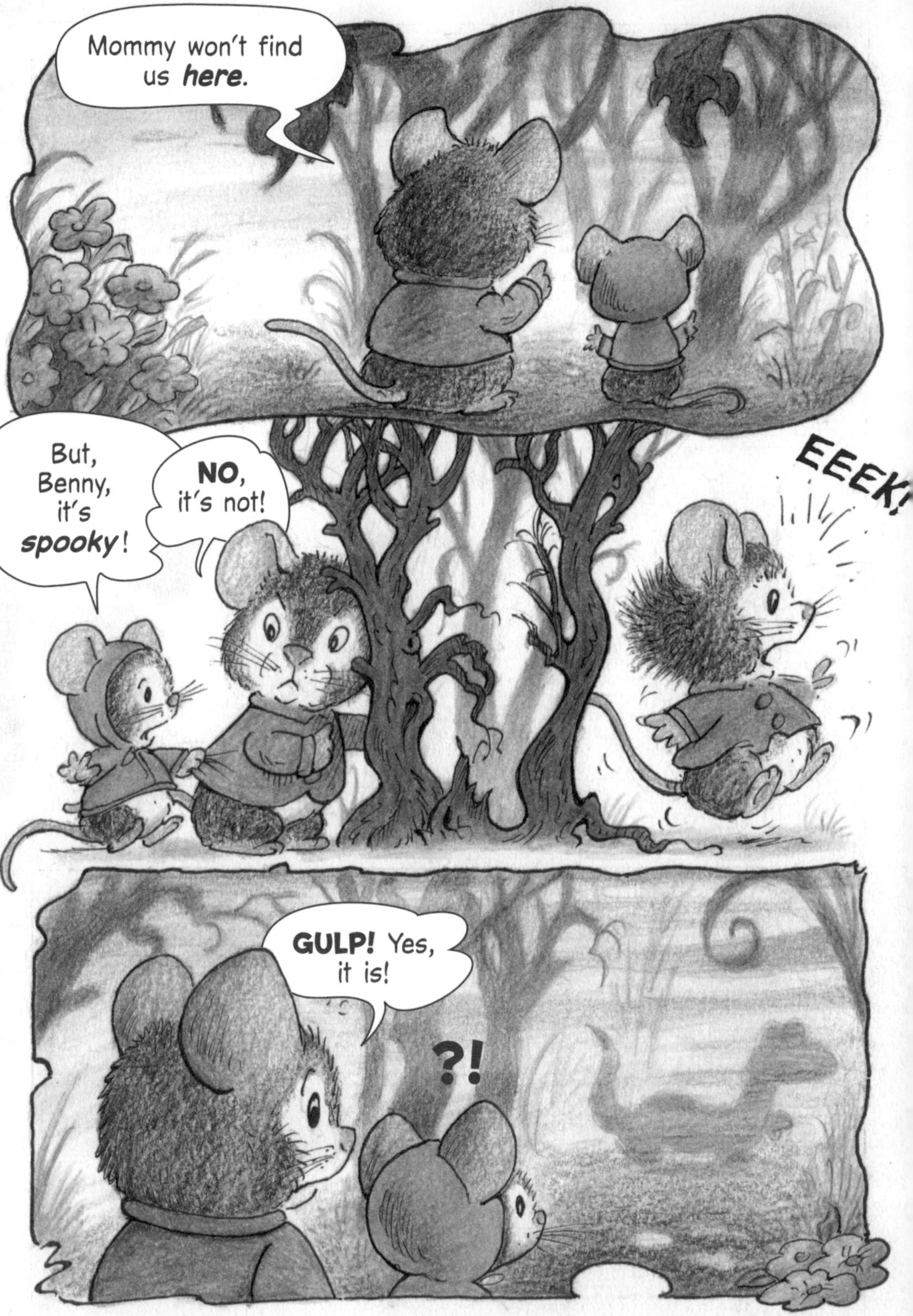
Mommy won't find us *here*.
But, Benny, it's *spooky*!
NO, it's not!
EEEK!
GULP! Yes, it is!
?!

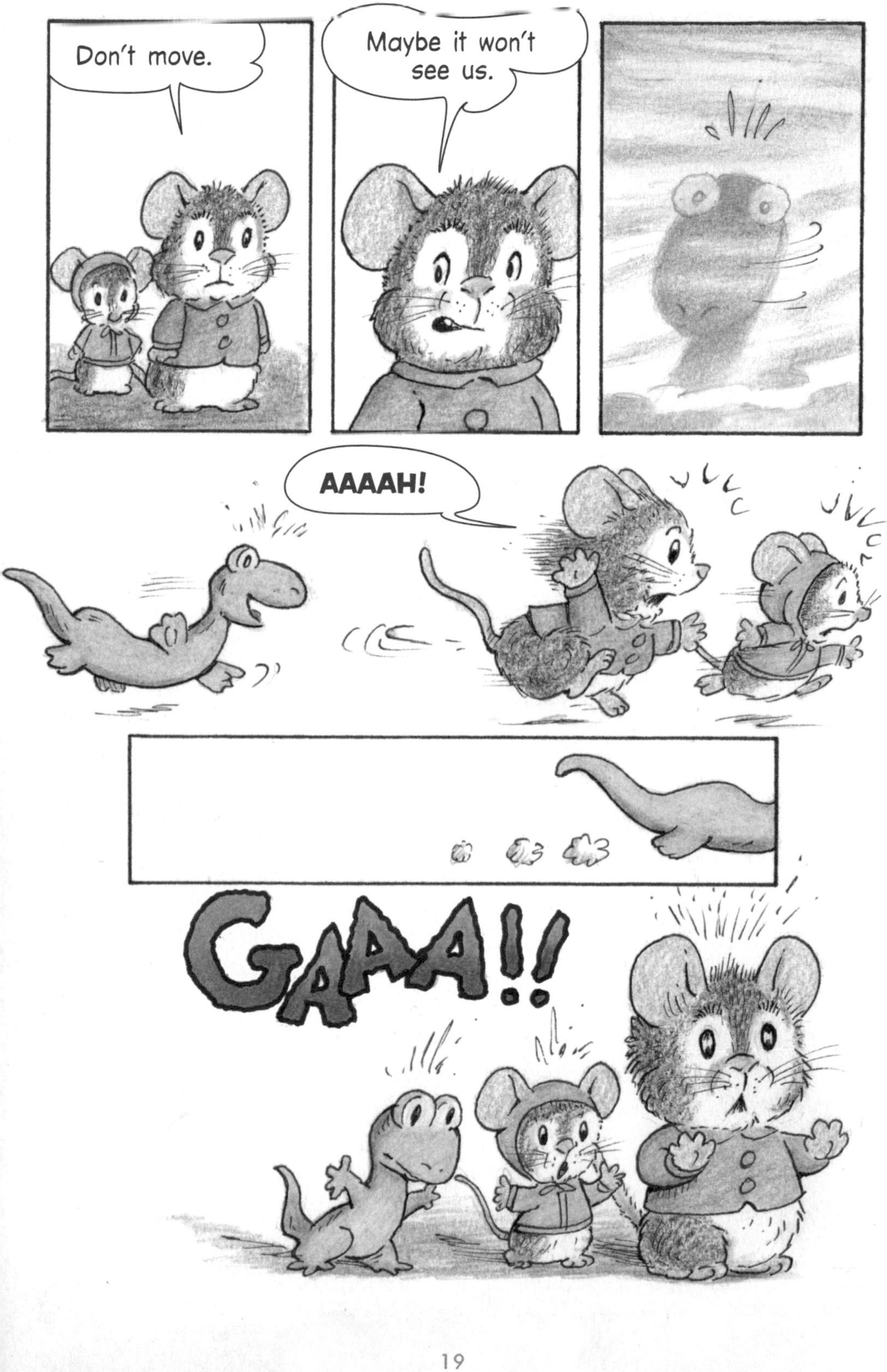
Don't move.
Maybe it won't see us.
AAAAH!
GAA!!

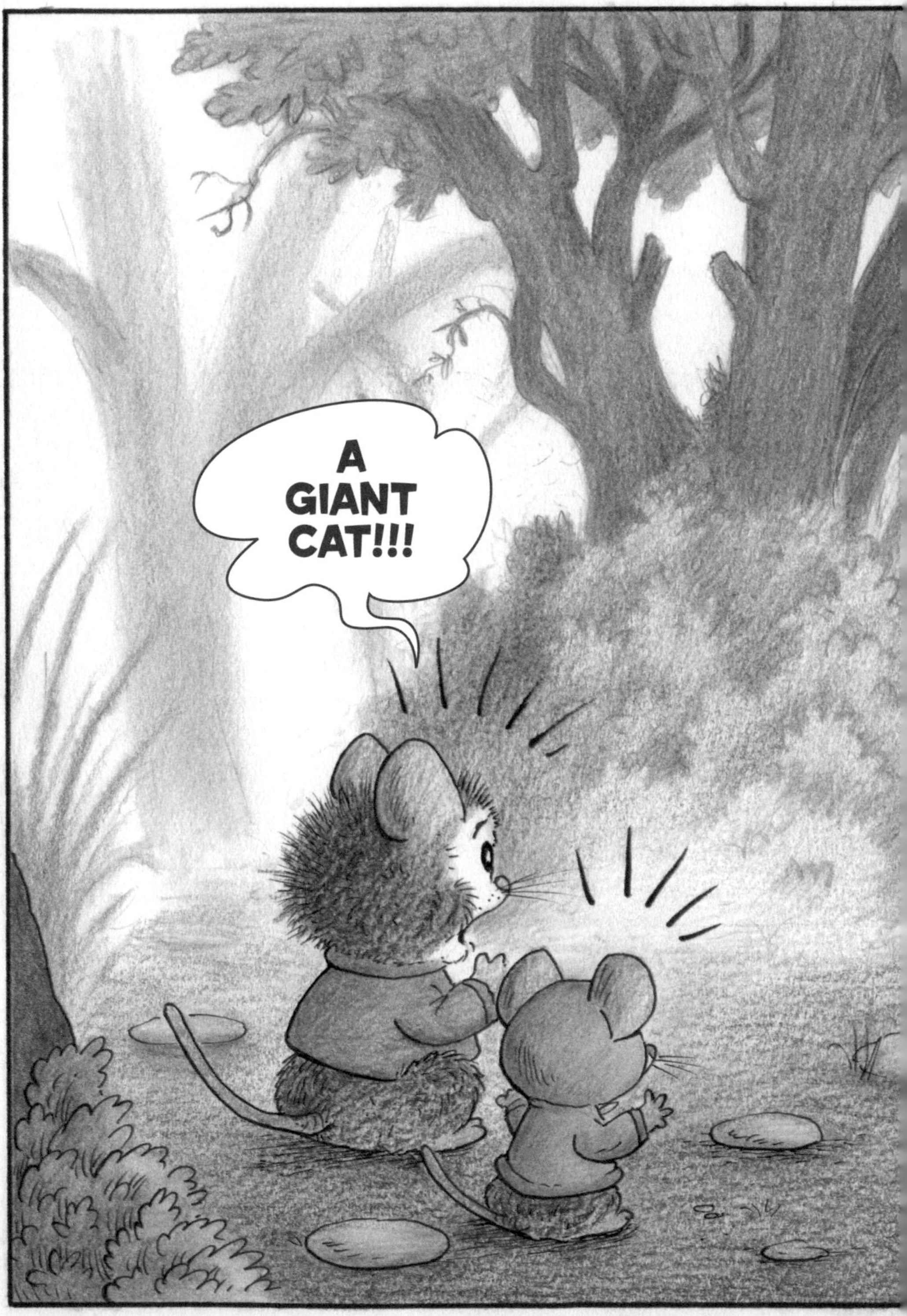
A GIANT CAT!!!

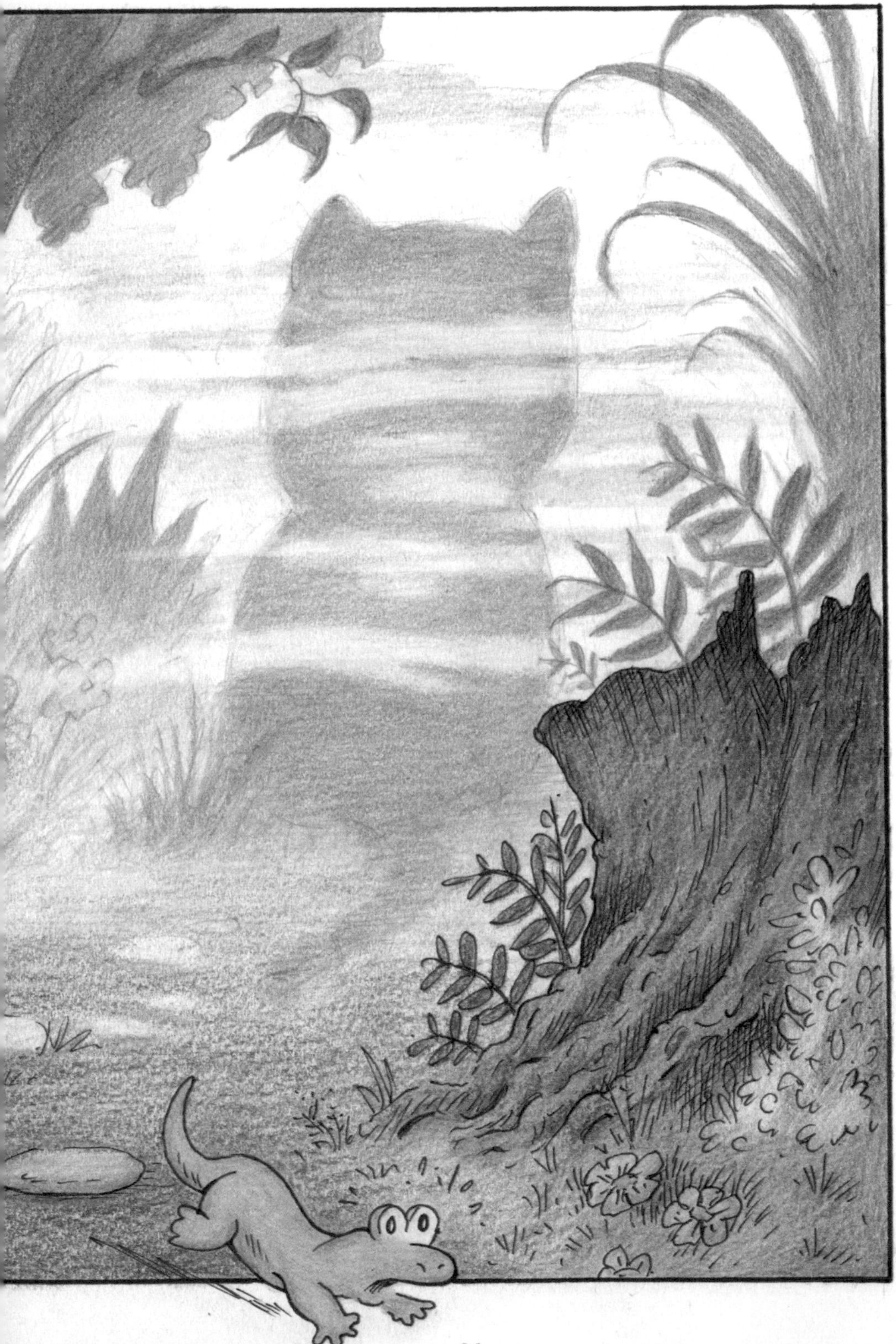

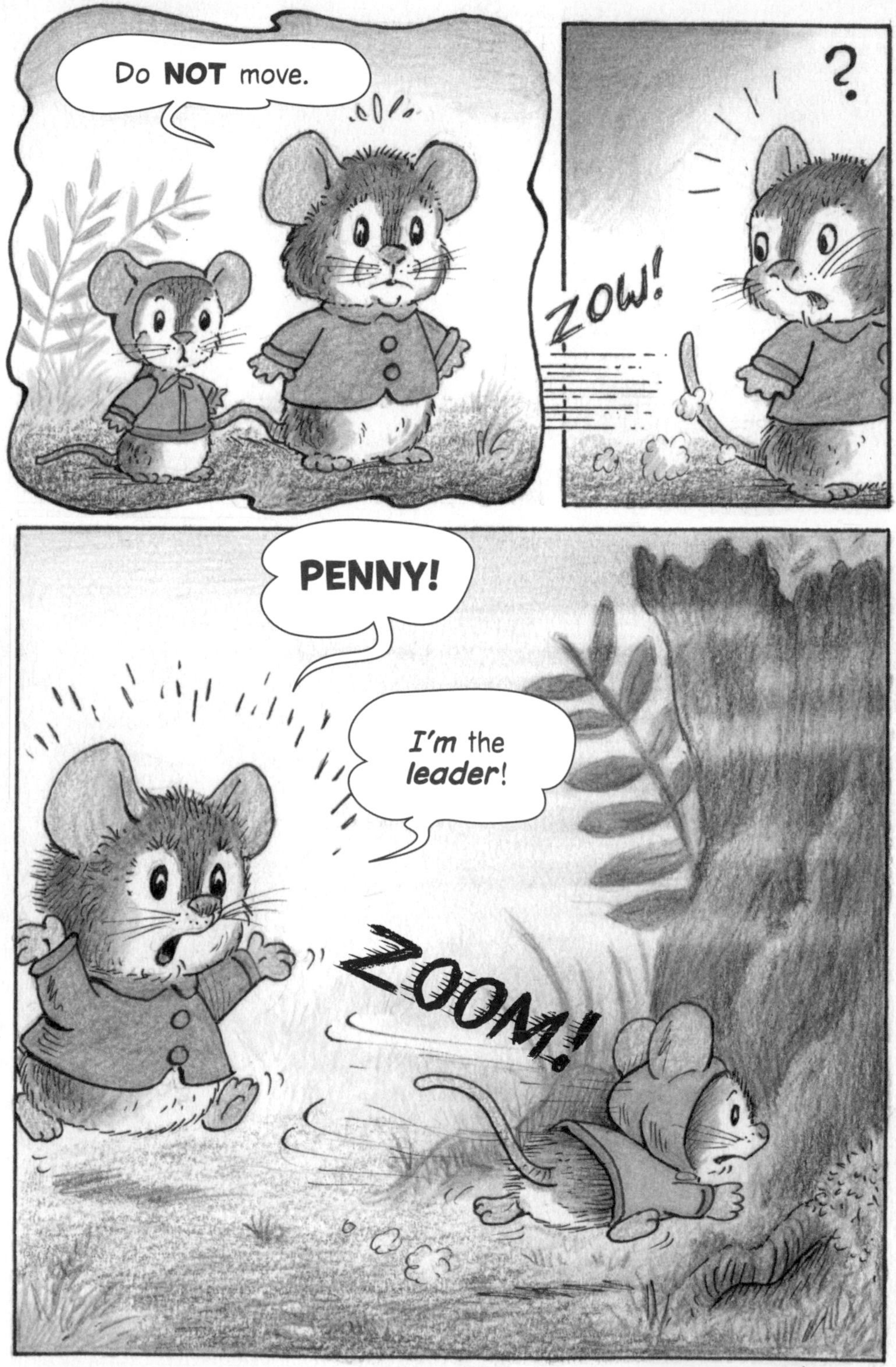
Do NOT move.
?
ZOW!
PENNY!
I'm the leader!
ZOOM!

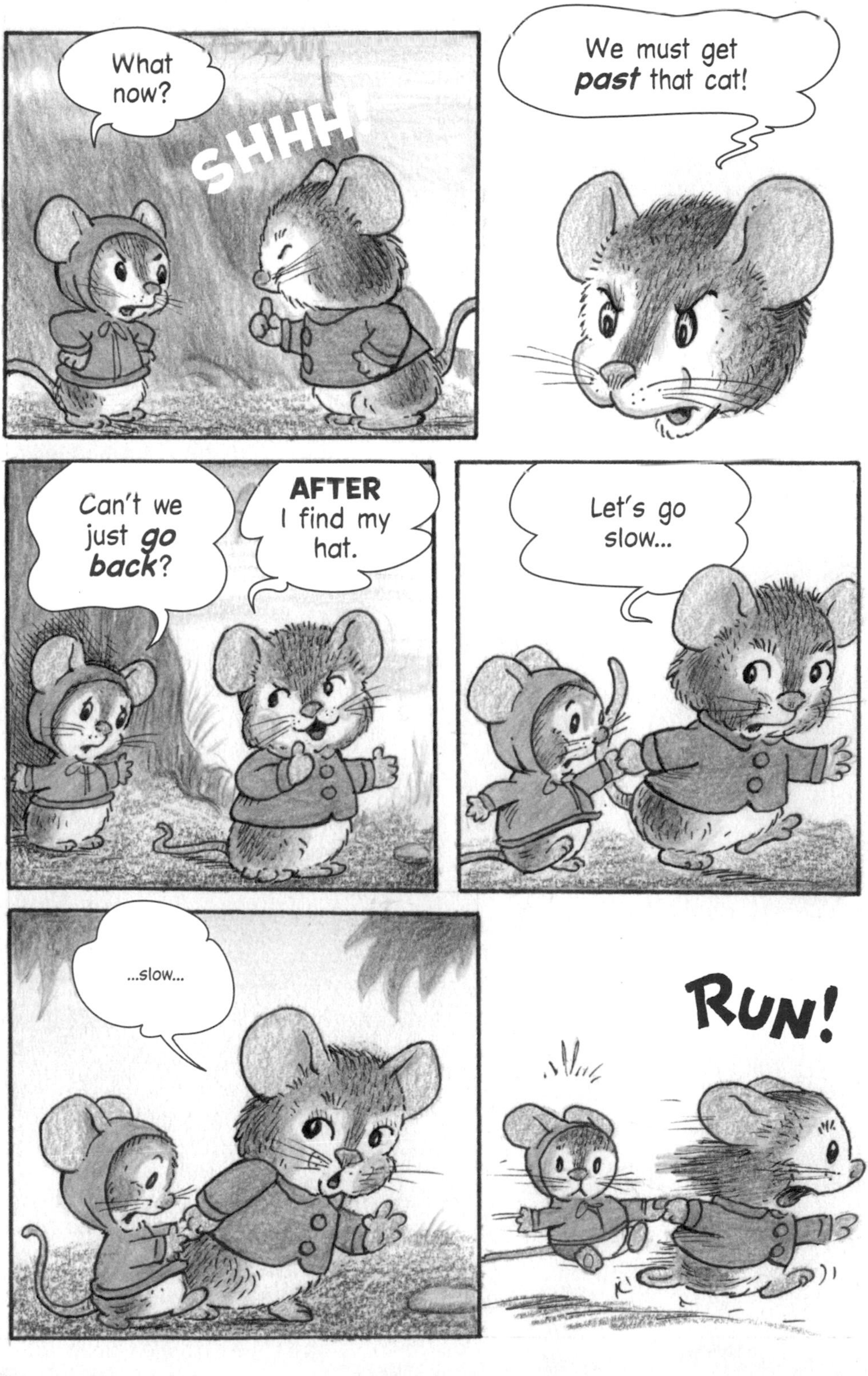
What now?
SHHH
We must get **past** that cat!
Can't we just **go back**?
AFTER I find my hat.
Let's go slow...
...slow...
RUN!

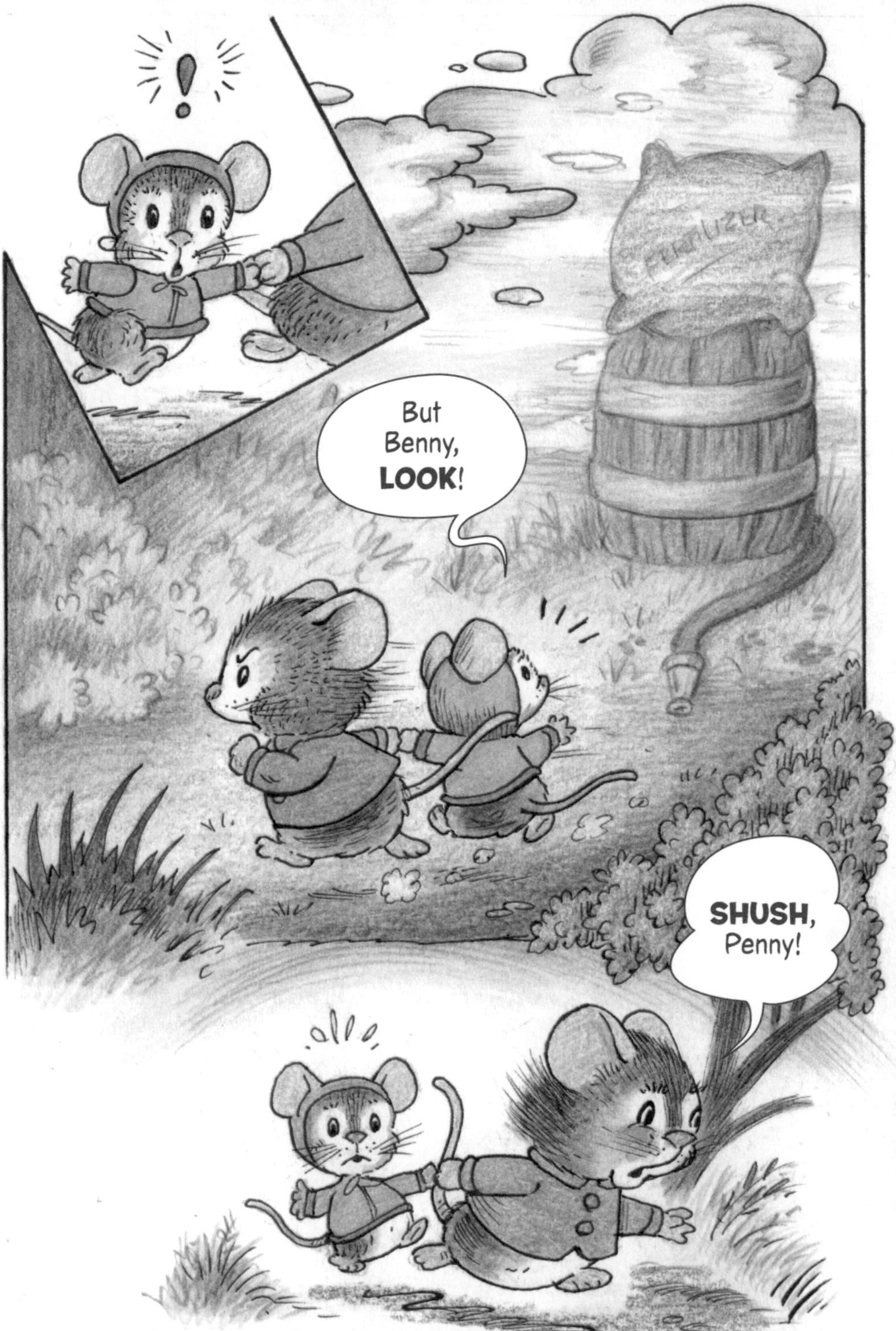
But Benny, **LOOK**!
SHUSH, Penny!

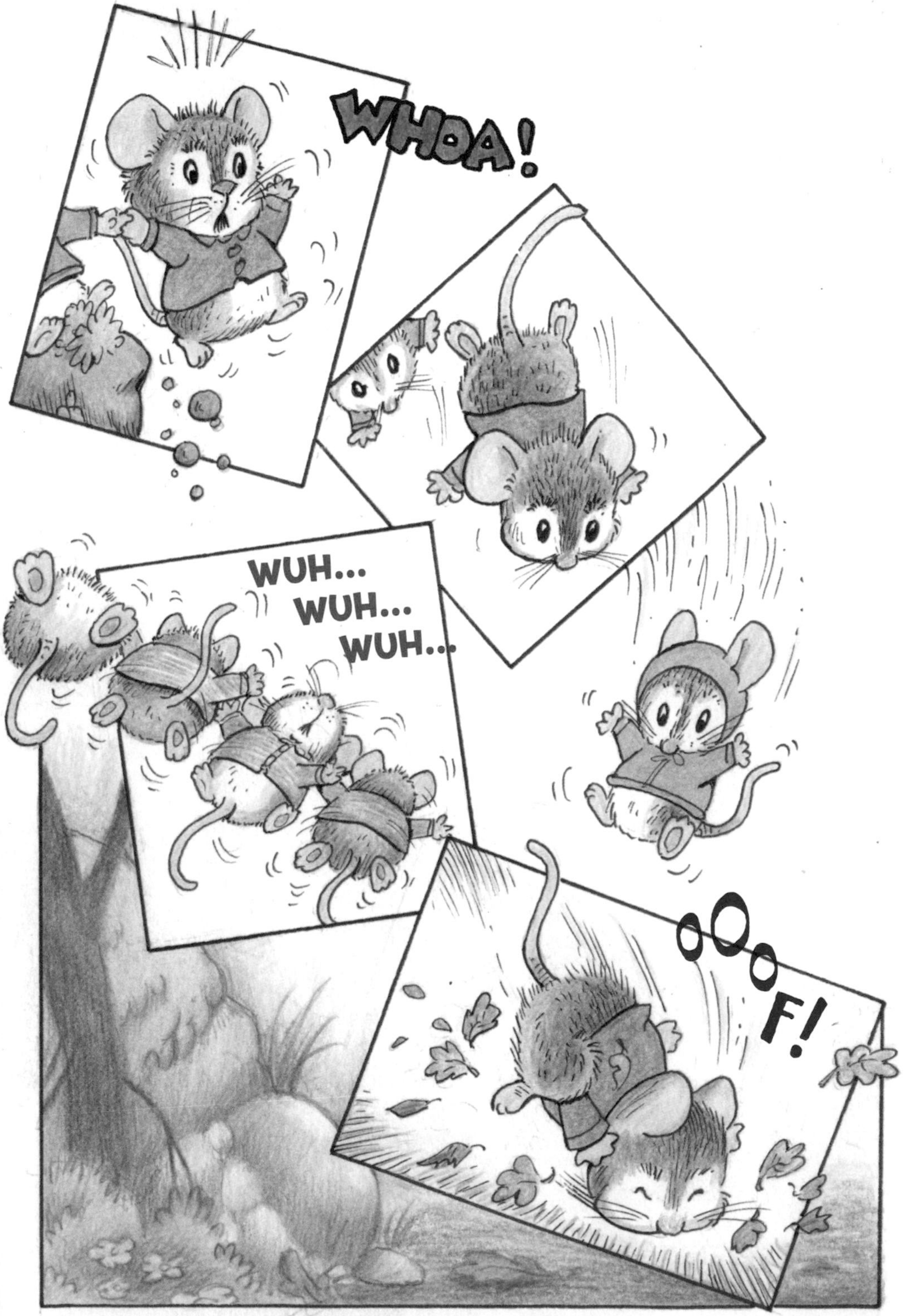
WHOA!
WUH...
WUH...
WUH...
OOOF!

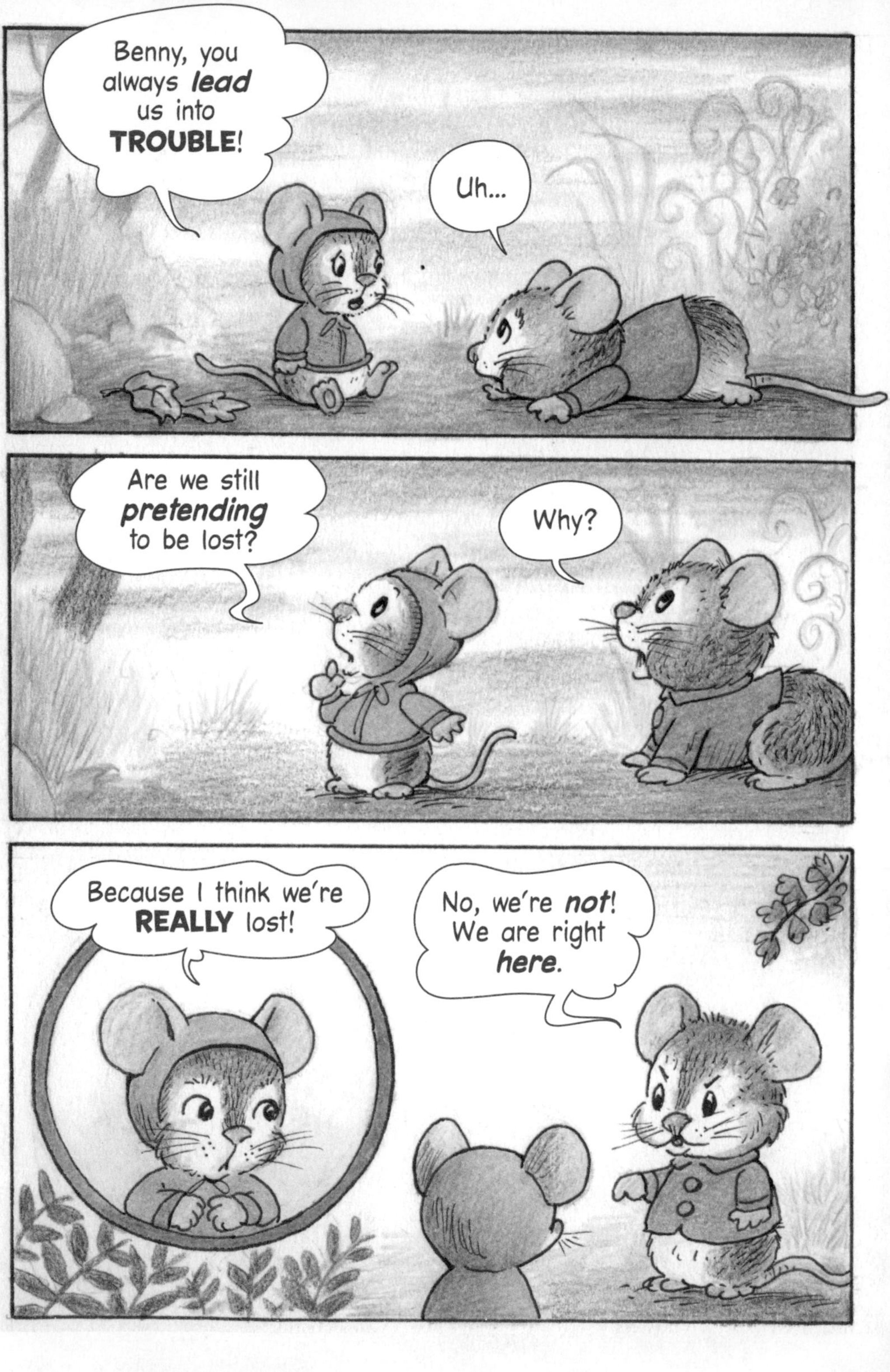
Benny, you always *lead* us into **TROUBLE**!
Uh...
Are we still *pretending* to be lost?
Why?
Because I think we're **REALLY** lost!
No, we're *not*! We are right *here*.

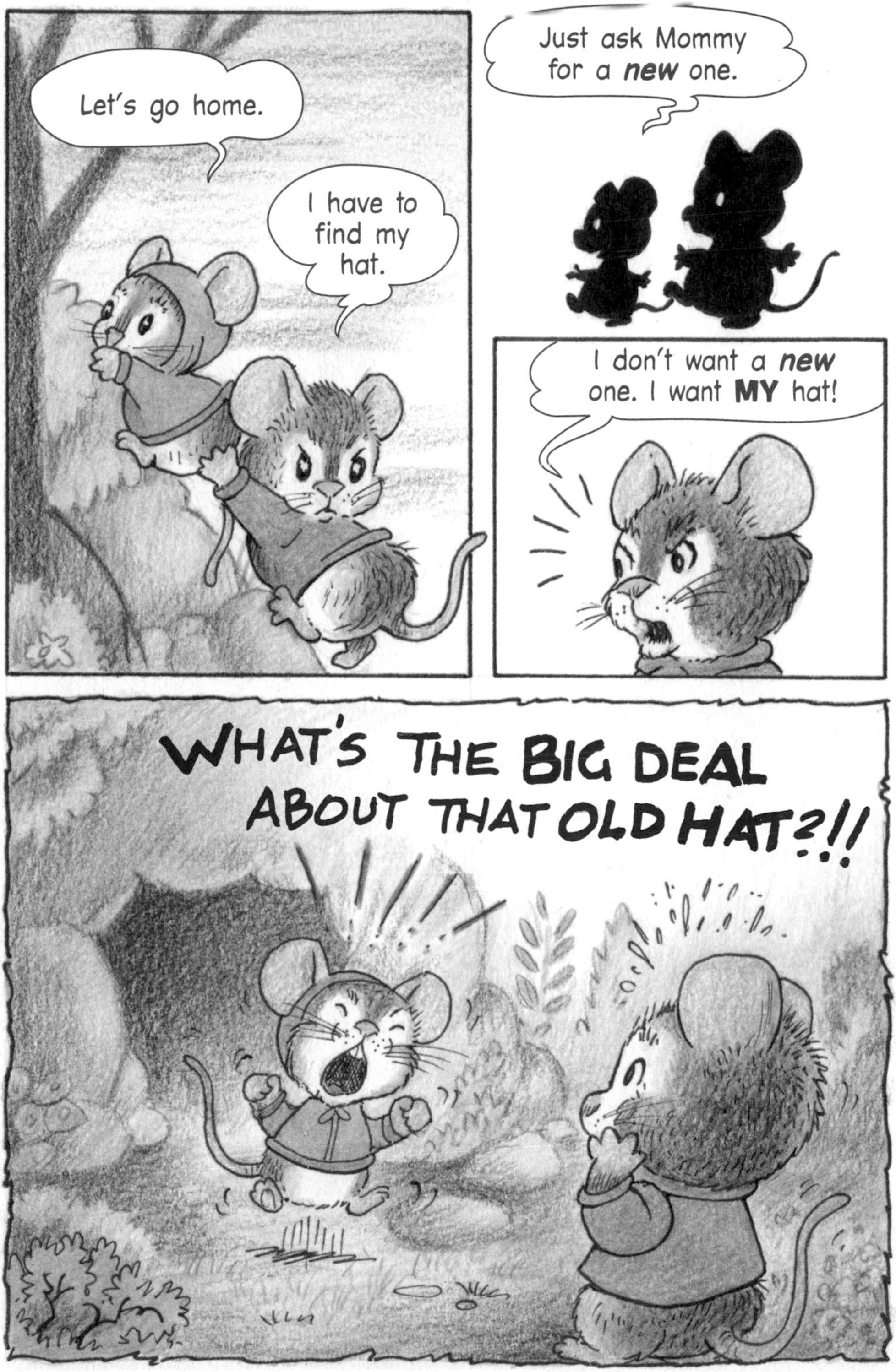
Let's go home.
I have to find my hat.
Just ask Mommy for a new one.
I don't want a new one. I want MY hat!
WHAT'S THE BIG DEAL ABOUT THAT OLD HAT?!!

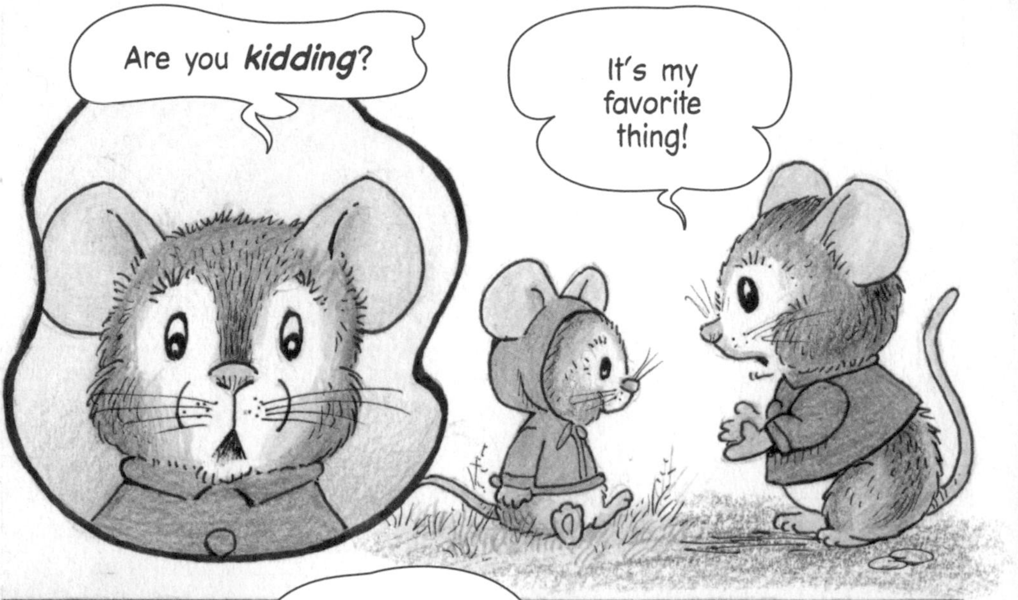
Are you ***kidding***?
It's my favorite thing!

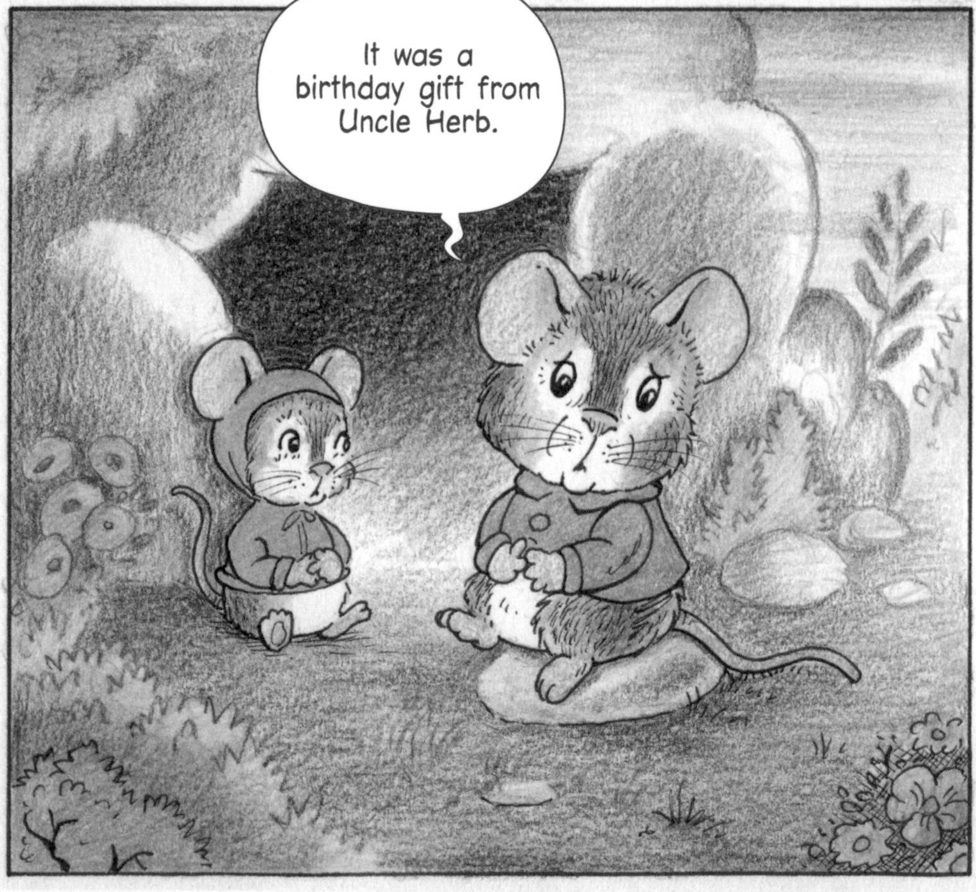
It was a birthday gift from Uncle Herb.

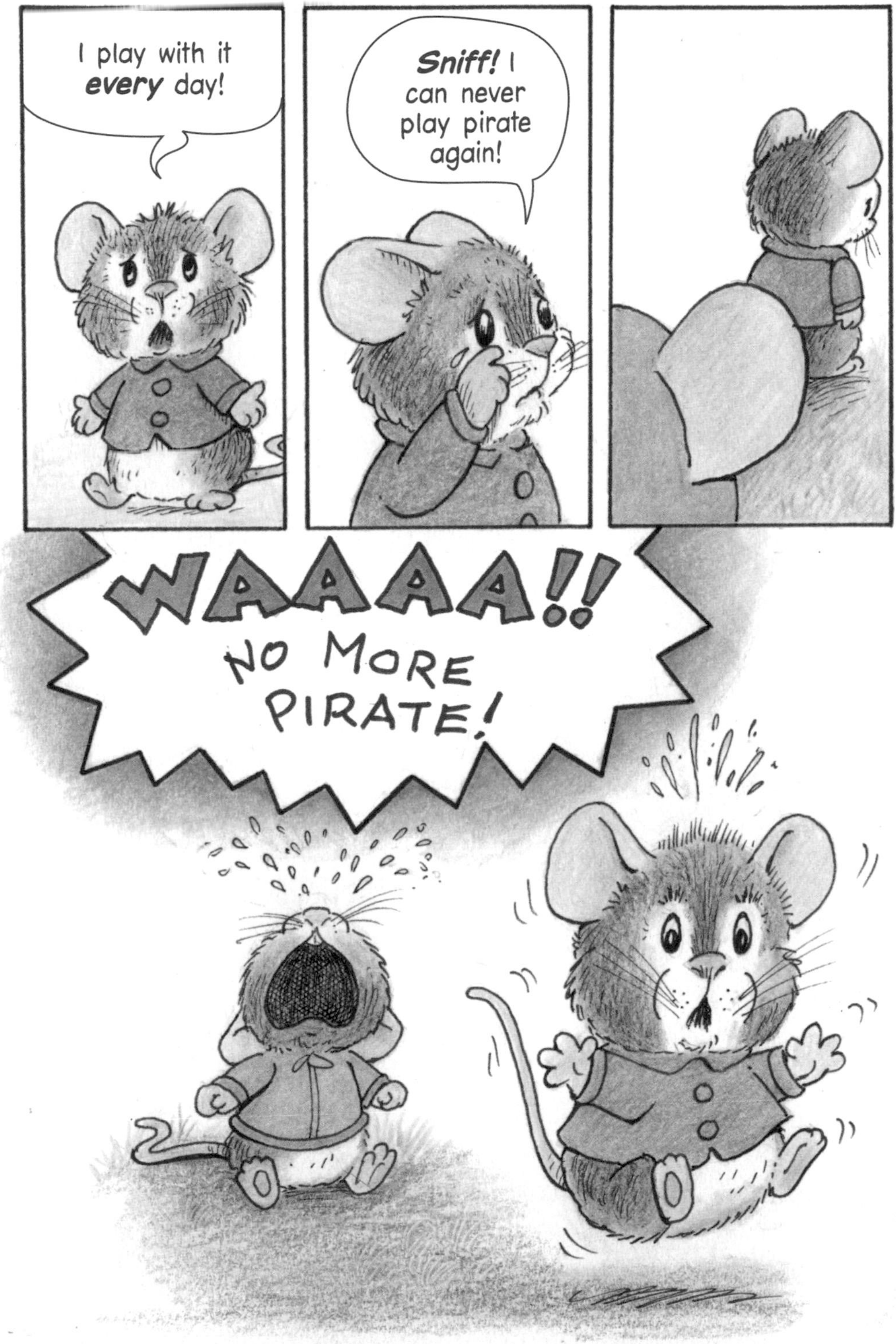
I play with it ***every*** day!
Sniff! I can never play pirate again!
WAAAA!!
NO MORE PIRATE!

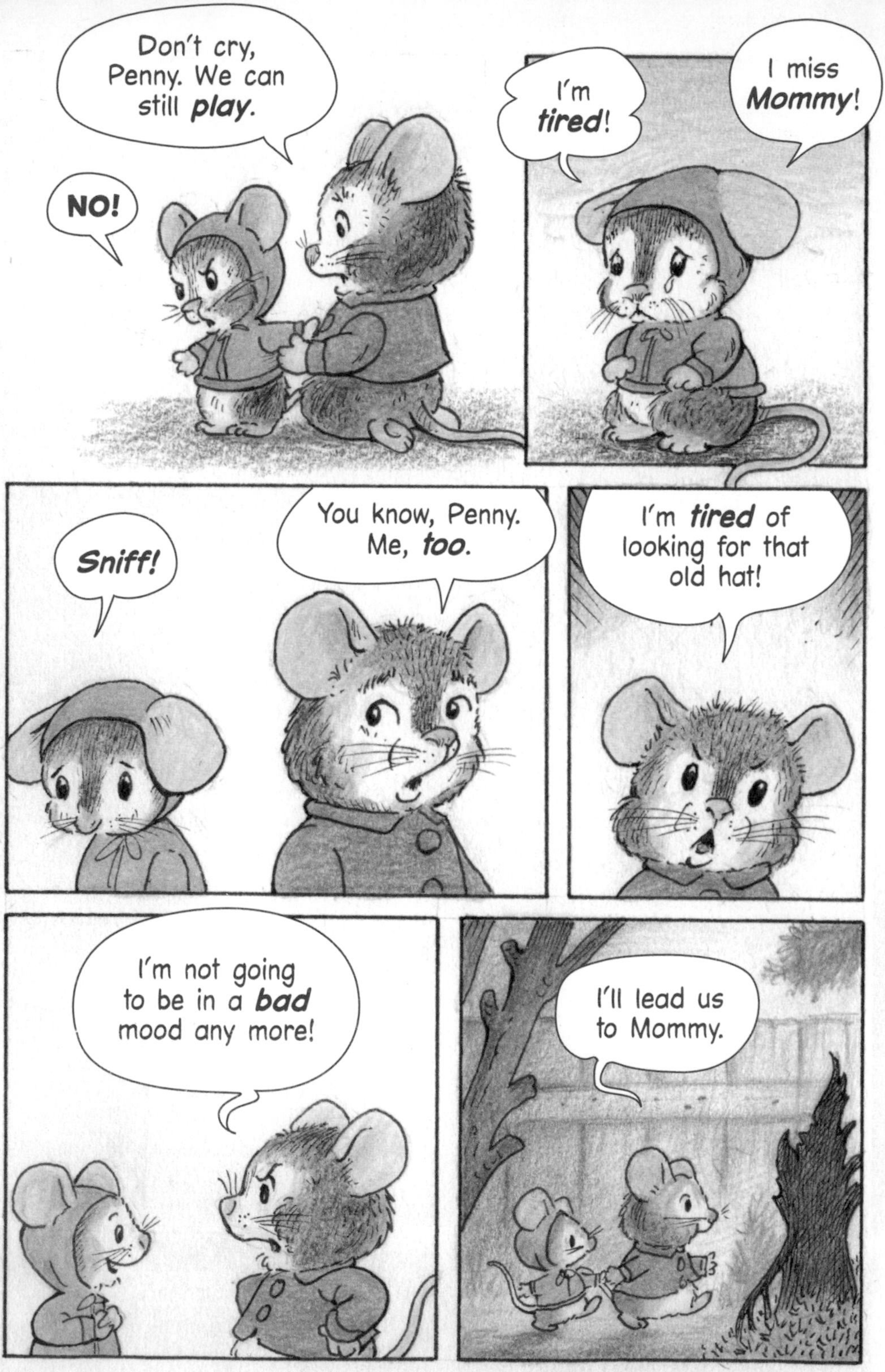
Don't cry, Penny. We can still *play*.
NO!
I'm *tired*!
I miss *Mommy*!
Sniff!
You know, Penny. Me, *too*.
I'm *tired* of looking for that old hat!
I'm not going to be in a *bad* mood any more!
I'll lead us to Mommy.

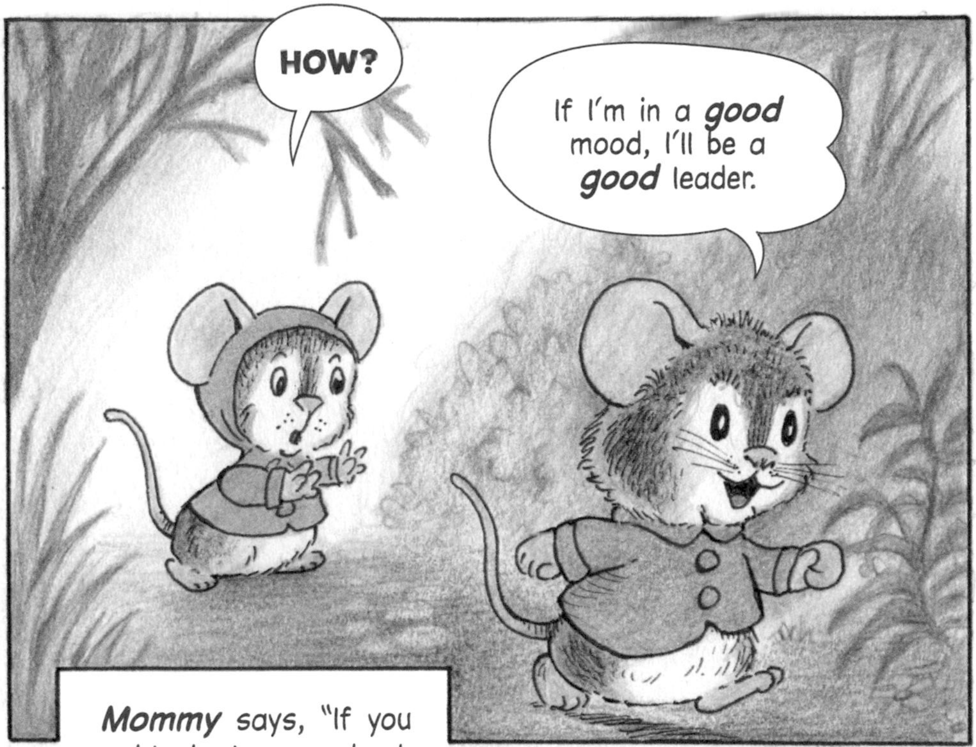
HOW?
If I'm in a *good* mood, I'll be a *good* leader.

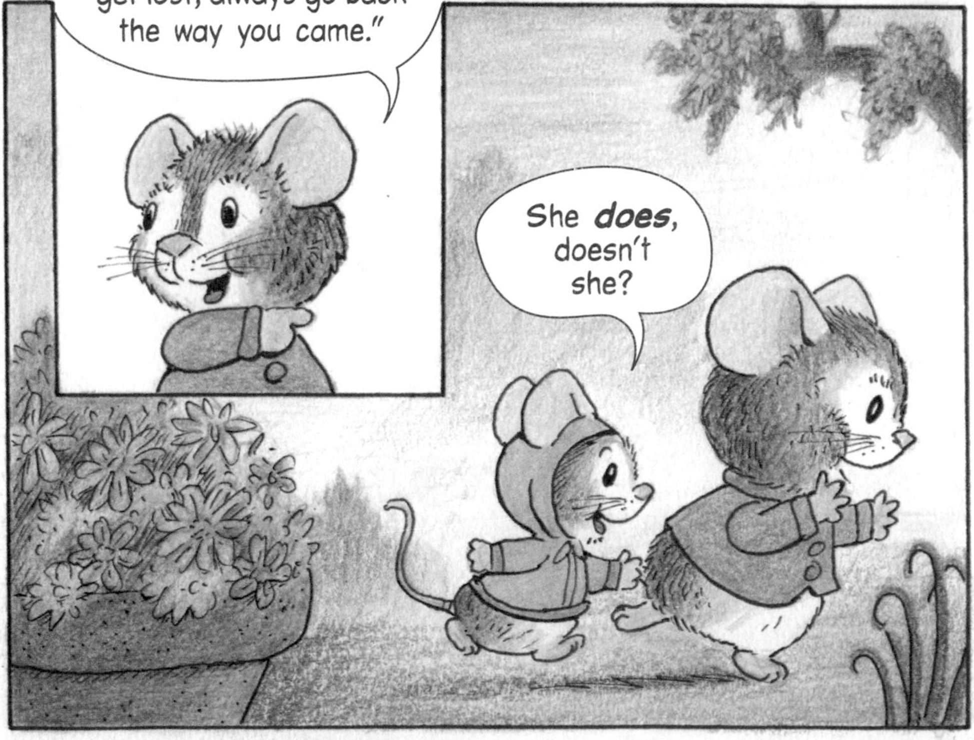
Mommy says, "If you get lost, always go back the way you came."
She *does*, doesn't she?

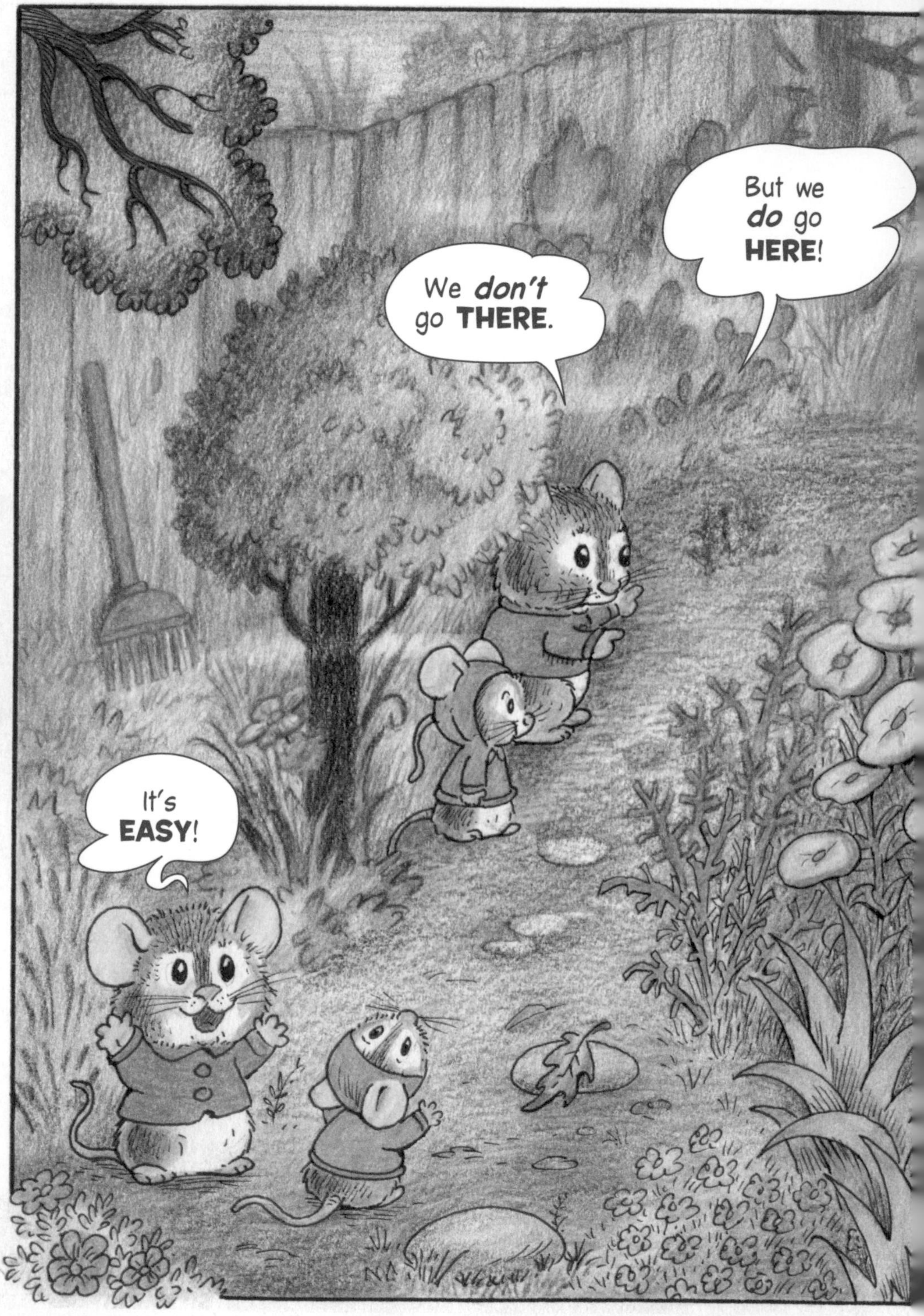
We don't go THERE.
But we do go HERE!
It's EASY!

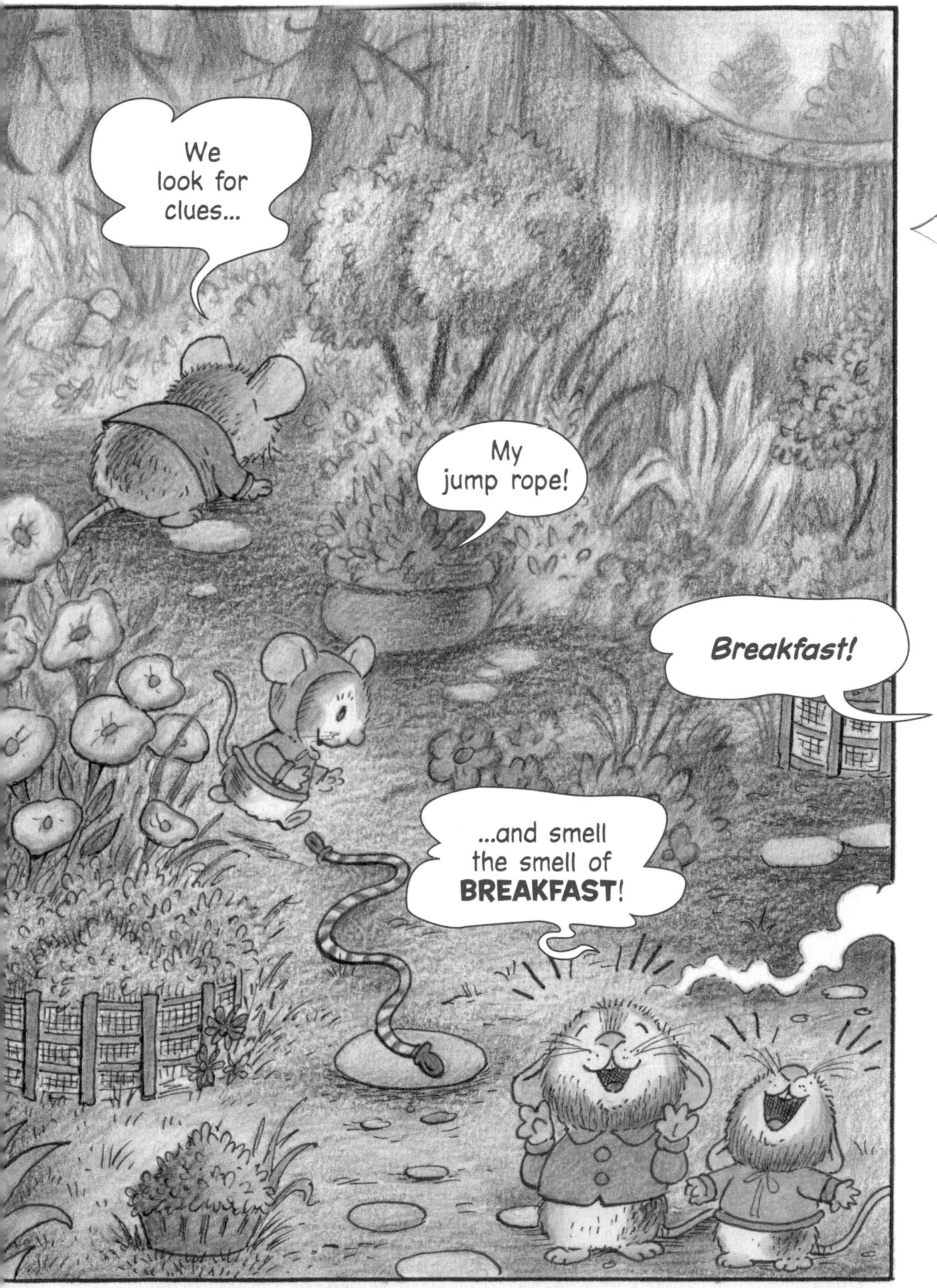
We look for clues...
My jump rope!
Breakfast!
...and smell the smell of BREAKFAST!

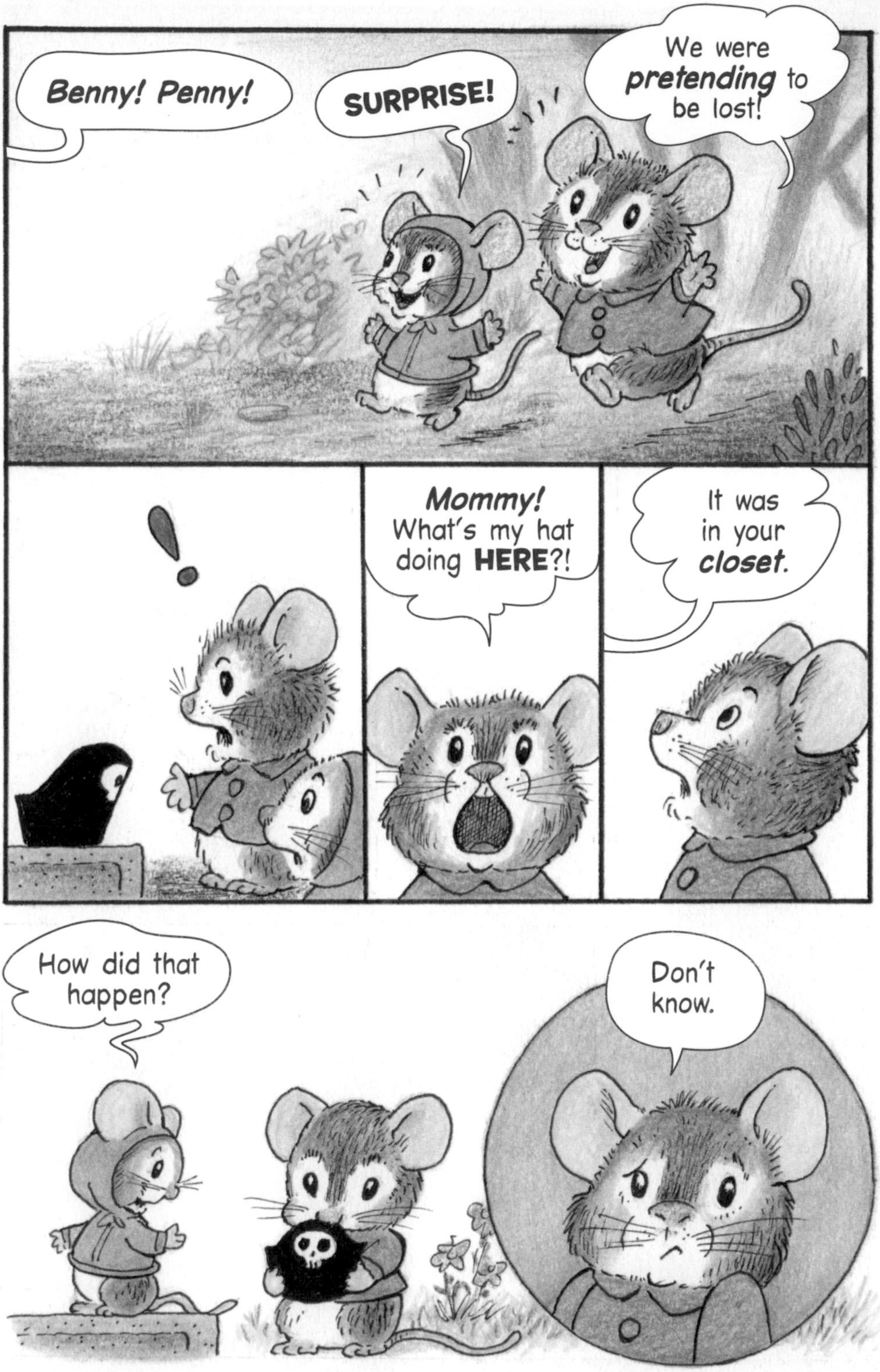
Benny! Penny!
SURPRISE!
We were pretending to be lost!
Mommy! What's my hat doing HERE?!
It was in your closet.
How did that happen?
Don't know.

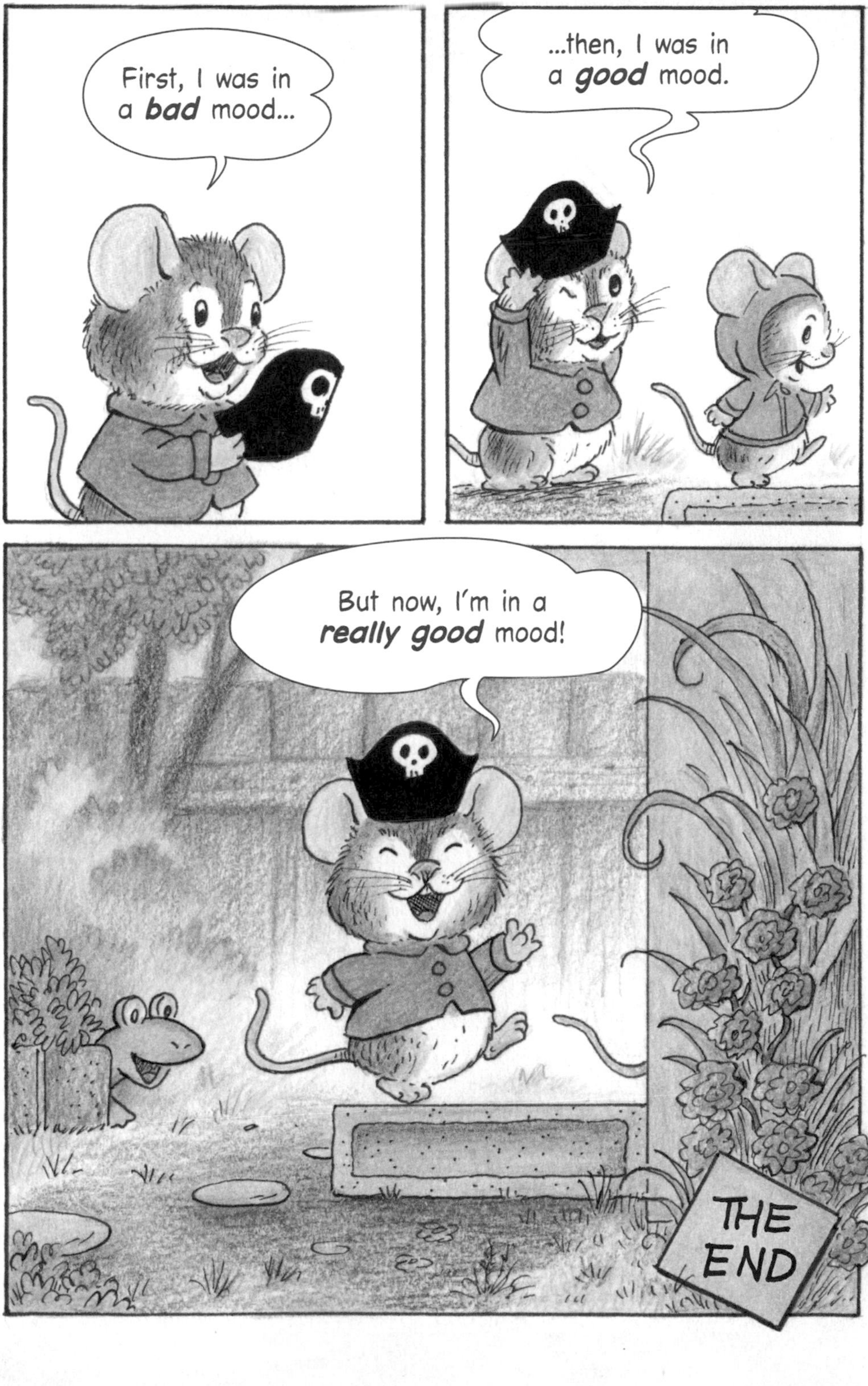
First, I was in a **bad** mood...
...then, I was in a **good** mood.
But now, I'm in a **really good** mood!
THE END

ABOUT THE AUTHOR

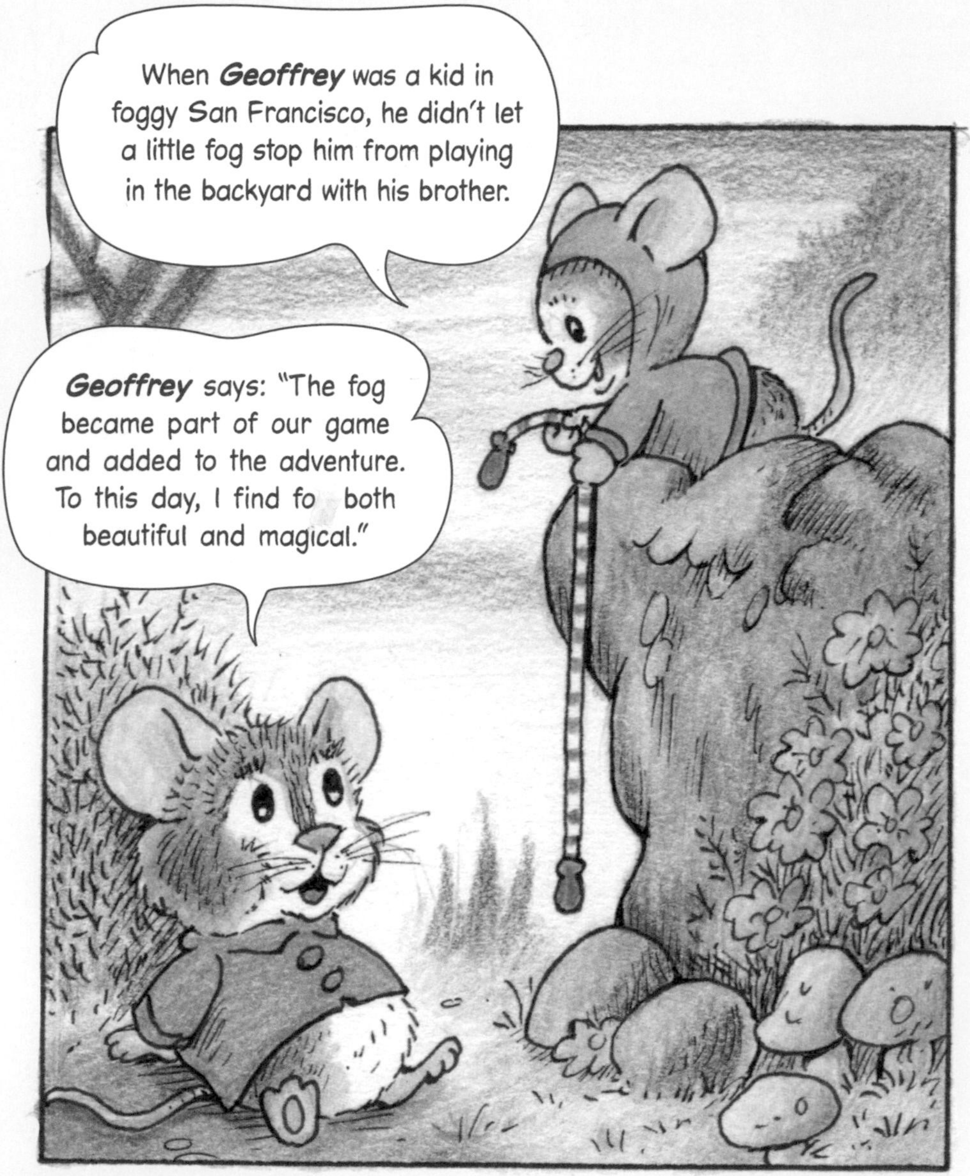
When *Geoffrey* was a kid in foggy San Francisco, he didn't let a little fog stop him from playing in the backyard with his brother.
Geoffrey says: "The fog became part of our game and added to the adventure. To this day, I find fo both beautiful and magical."

GEOFFREY HAYES is the author/illustrator of the Patrick Brown books and of the successful series of early readers Otto and Uncle Tooth. His best-selling TOON Books series, Benny and Penny, has garnered multiple awards including the Theodor Seuss Geisel Award, given to "the most distinguished American book for beginning readers published during the preceding year."